The dictatress of Cyclops announced:

"The respected representative from Zarathustra Refugee Planet One suggested a lever to oust the Corps Galactica from its role of policy-maker in this area. I have come to an inescapable conclusion that it is not consistent with our ideals to tolerate the Corps's presence here while they are flouting our wishes.

"I therefore wish to inform you that I am serving notice today on the base's commandant to withdraw all Corps personnel from Cyclops and close the base. From this moment forward the base will be quarantined. . . ."

But the operatives of the Corps knew that what she was concealing was the one interplanetary crime which could not be tolerated by the community of civilized worlds.

A.P. VAN DOREN

THE REPAIRMEN OF CYCLOPS

John Brunner

DAW Books, Inc.
Donald A. Wollheim, Publisher
1633 Broadway, New York, N.Y. 10019

Printing History: A slightly shorter version of this novel appeared as a serial in *Fantastic Stories,* copyright © 1965 by Ziff-Davis Publishing Company. This version was reprinted in a paperback edition, copyright © 1965 by Ace Books, Inc.; the rights therein reverted to the author in 1971. The present version has been revised for this 1981 edition.

FIRST DAW PRINTING, JULY 1981

1 2 3 4 5 6 7 8 9

 DAW TRADEMARK REGISTERED
U.S. PAT. OFF. MARCA
REGISTRADA. HECHO EN U.S.A.

PRINTED IN U.S.A.

I

The sky rang with the reverberation of fierce white sunlight like the interior of a blue drum. Wind hot as the breath of a furnace teased the silver ocean into ripples, and the ripples shattered the sun's image into a blazing pathway of diamond fragments. Itching with sweat, aching with tension, Justin Kolb had to narrow his eyes even behind his wholeface visor because the response-limit of the glass was exceeded if he turned his head towards that glistening track over the water and the opacity curve took a sudden dive towards complete blankness.

Maddeningly, it was to sunward that he had caught the first wing-glints.

He had expected that the sight of the Jackson's buzzards would crystallise his formless tension into the old familiar excitement, re-unite mind and body into the efficient combination, as much weapon as person, which was Justin Kolb at peak operational efficiency. He had been trying for so long to get away on his own like this, on the hunter's trail which now had to make do for his old, preferred pastimes, that the strain of habituation to waiting had soured his keen anticipation of the chase.

Only till I see the buzzards, he had promised himself. *And then—*

But he'd seen the buzzards at last, when he had half decided he was too far north even at this season, two days past midsummer, and the instant of thrill had been—an instant. Now he was back in the slough of dreary awareness which had plagued him the whole of yesterday and the whole of the day before. He was conscious of suffocating heat, of blinding brightness, of prickling perspiration, of cramp from keeping the skimmer level and aligned despite the tug of the waves. His hands were slippery on the controls, and the hard butt of his harpoon-gun seemed to take up twice as much room on the skimmer's deck as it usually did.

Briefly, he shut his eyes, wishing with all his force that somehow time could turn back and he could be free to return to space.

Cyclops, though, was a relatively poor world. It could not support luxury spaceflight. Out there, a man had to be productive—mining asteroids, servicing solar power relays, doing some clock-around job with the absolute concentration of machinery.

What the hell am I now? A gigolo.

The thought passed. True or not, he was at least able to indulge this much of his thirst for excitement and challenge; if he had taken any other of the courses open to him, he would have been drudging away this glorious summer in a city or on a farm or in some squalid fishing-port, pestered continually by the demands of other people, by the need to stack up work-credits, by holes in his shoes or leaks in his roof.

Even her high-and-mightiness is preferable to that . . .

He blinked. The wing-glints had come again, and this time remained in view instead of vanishing into the blur of heat-haze and shimmery reflection along the skyline. His pulse beat faster as he began to count: five, six—eight, ten, at least a dozen and possibly more.

Name of the cosmos, but it must be a giant!

For one moment, uncharacteristic alarm filled him. He had come deliberately to this northern extreme of the wolfsharks' range, because those that beat a path of slaughter more than a hundred miles from the equatorial shallows which were their customary habitat were certain to be the largest and greediest specimens, and after his long impatient chafing in Frecity he had felt nothing less than a monster would compensate him.

But seeing a dozen or more buzzards hovering was a shock.

It was perhaps the most characteristic sight on Cyclops: Jackson's buzzards, swift, cruel-taloned, steely-winged, on the track of a wolfshark, which killed for savage delight and not for hunger, so that even the monstrous appetites of the birds were easily glutted by its gore-leaking victims. At this time of year, nearer the equator, one could look out over the sea and espy as many as five or six groups of the carrion-eaters following the blood-smeared killers, for the ocean teemed with life.

Yet it was rare to see more than six buzzards to every wolfshark. By twos and threes, they would sate themselves and flap heavily away, while others took their place, the total number in the sky remaining roughly constant. And there were reasons why those that roamed furthest north were followed usually only by two or three buzzards: first, the sea offered fewer victims and hence less carrion; second, the birds were still feeding their young at this time of year, and could not wander too far from their breeding-mats, the vast raft-like assemblies of Cyclops kelp which occurred only in a narrow belt around the planet's centre.

Nonetheless, here it was: a wolfshark so big, so fast, and so murderous that a hundred miles away from home it was killing in quantities great enough to tip the balance in the buzzards' dim minds on the side of greed rather than loyalty to their offspring.

He pursed his lips and eased his harpoon-gun closer to the firing-notch out in the forward gunwale of the skimmer. Would one shot do the job? Would it be better to load first with an unlined harpoon, to weaken the killer, before risking a shot with line attached and the consequent danger of being dragged to the bottom? Had this enormous beast been attacked and escaped before—if it had, how many times? The more often, the warier it would be of an approaching skimmer, and the more likely it would be to attack even if there was easy prey closer to hand.

He weighed possibilities with half his mind, while with the other half he reviewed the area where he found himself.

This was the water-hemisphere of Cyclops, insofar as the differentiation was meaningful. It was a shallow-sea planet—its moon being rather small, and incapable of raising large tides either in the crustal material or in the oceans, although its sun exerted considerable tidal influence.

The shallowness of the sea, combined with a total volume of water close to the average for Class A planets (those on which human beings could survive, eating some of the vegetation and at least a few of the native animals) meant that the dry-land area was chopped up into small sections. The other half of the planet boasted some quite sizeable islands, and even a quasi-continent consisting of a score of large islands linked by isthmuses. This side was sparsely inhabited, and the largest island within hundreds of miles was officially not even part of Cyclops, but a repair and recreation base for the Corps Galactica.

A certain amount of fishing; a certain amount of scrap-reclamation; some terrafarms on islands isolated enough to be worth maintaining as pure-human ecological units against the risk of drifting seeds and wandering fauna from the Cyclops-normal islands around them— that was the sum of human engagement with this hemisphere, apart from solar and tidal power installations operating with a minimum of manned supervision.

Kolb hesitated. Then he gave a harsh laugh. Was he going to let the risk of dying alone and far from rescue prevent him from going after this record-breaking wolf-shark? He would never be able to face his image in the mirror again!

In any case, out in space he had faced death not hundreds, but hundreds of thousands of miles from the nearest other humans.

His mind darkened briefly. He never cared to recall the circumstances that had brought him back from space to a planet-bound existence, and forbidden him to combine his lust for danger with valuable work. There was nothing of value to anyone but himself in this single-handed hunting; men had shared Cyclops with wolf-sharks for long enough to determine the limits within which they could be a nuisance, and if the necessity arose, the species was culled efficiently and with precision by teams working from the air.

In fact, thought Kolb greyly, *there's damned little value to anybody in anything I've done with my life lately. Least of all to me . . .*

Slowly, as the wing-glints came closer, following a line that would pass him within some four or five miles and if extended would eventually approach the island where the Corps Galactica maintained its repair base, a kind of muted exultation filled him. He could see now that the buzzards were too full already to make more than token swoops on what the wolfshark killed, yet—as though admiring the energy of the beast—they none of them made to flap back to the south and their breeding-mats.

It'll break all the records. I never even heard of such a giant!

He put aside the unlined harpoon which his hand had automatically sought for the first shot. With fingers as exact as a surgeon's, he loaded a harpoon with line attached, and laid the gun in its firing-notch.

Then he closed his left hand on the control levers, and without a tremor fed power to the reactor.

The skimmer leapt up on its planes with a shriek loud enough to startle a wolfshark at twice this range, and instantly the wheeling buzzards disgorged the last food they had eaten and climbed a safe hundred feet into the sky. Just audible over the thrum of power from his craft, Kolb heard their whickering cries, like the neighing of frightened horses.

And one of his questions was answered, anyway. This wolfshark had been attacked before, often enough to recognise a skimmer for the danger it represented. It forgot its business of stitching a line of destruction across the peaceful ocean, and spun around in the water to confront the fragile boat. It lowered its tail and spread its fans, and its head rose to the surface.

Kolb's self-possession wavered, so that he had to cling desperately to his unverbalised decision: *it doesn't matter if I die or not!* Thinking of it as huge, and seeing how huge it was, were two different things.

How big, then? Fifty feet from fan-tip to fan-tip, oscillating in the water like a manta ray, but having a tapered body which was all keel for the muscles driving those fans, perfectly streamlined; a mere twitch, a single shrug of those muscles would hurl it torpedo-swift on anything else which swam the waters of Cyclops, and jaws which could open to engulf a man would clamp serrated rows of fangs into, and *through*, the victim. The bite killed, and the killer forgot. In summer, it was never hungry. It swallowed what its jaws held, and that sufficed until the next kill, minutes later.

Kolb silenced the yammering alarms in his mind and lined up the sights of his gun rock-steady on the centre of the maw.

And then, with the distance closing to two hundred yards, a hundred and fifty, there came the boom.

It rocked the skimmer. It startled the wolfshark. It was the noise of a Corps Galactica spacecraft braking at the edge of atmosphere to put down at the repair base.

By a reflex not even the danger of death could overrule, ex-spaceman Justin Kolb glanced up, and the sun shone full on his wholeface visor, triggering and overloading the glare response, so that he was blind. He cried out, his hand closing on the trigger of his gun. The harpoon whistled wide of a target, and the wolfshark charged.

II

During the flight Maddalena Santos had mostly sat staring at nothing, turning over and over in her mind the decision which now confronted her: to stay on, or not, in the Patrol Service.

Three other passengers were aboard—personnel from an airless Corps base further out towards the limits of the explored galaxy, on rotating local leave and very excited about it. Two of them were men. The fact that these men looked at her once only told her something about the effect of the last twenty years on her appearance.

It was one thing to know that she was assured of another two centuries of life. It was another to realise on this first visit to civilisation in so long a time how deep the impact of two decades on a barbarian world had gone.

She was assured of her longevity by the Patrol's payscale; in a galaxy where the older worlds were so rich it literally made no difference whether a given individual worked or not, it required either accidental dedication or a tempting bait to enlist volunteers for the necessary drudgery of governmental service.

Not that you can really call it government, Maddalena reminded herself listlessly. *It's more like herding cattle. And lazy cattle, at that.*

The other branches of government service paid at lower rates; only the Patrol paid ten-for-one in the unique currency of life.

She had served twenty years as an on-planet agent, among stinking barbarians lost in a mud-wallow, and she was entitled—if she chose to take it here and now—to a guaranteed two centuries of comfortable, healthy life, anywhere she chose. She could even go clear back to Earth, for she had been born there.

Wistfully, she looked at the black star-spangled backdrop of space, wondering what had happened on the mother world in the period she had been away.

She had been so optimistic . . . Right at the beginning of her career, when she was making out so badly in the Corps that she risked not even being promoted lieutenant from her initial probationer status—and hence losing forever her chance at longevity-payment—she had saved everything and indeed acquired some small reputation by a successful coup on a barbarian planet: one of the isolated Zarathustra Refugee Planets where fugitives had survived after fleeing the hell of the Zarathustra nova more than seven centuries previous.

But when she was offered a post as an on-planet agent, supervising and watching the progress of these stranded outcasts of humanity, since she was not permitted to return to the world where she had stirred up such a to-do, she had had to pick almost at random from the existing four or five vacancies.

And she had realised quite shortly after being assigned her post, in which the minimum stay was twenty years, that she had chosen wrong.

It had seemed that something was going to happen on the planet she selected—a transition from the typical mud-grubbing peasant level where many of the refugees had got stuck, to an expanding phase of incipient civilisation, with some industrialisation and a great deal of cross-cultural influence: fascinating material to study at first-hand.

But that occurrence depended on the survival of an organisational genius who had inherited the headship of a strategically sited city-state. And within a month of her arrival, one of his jealous rivals assassinated him and seized power, condemning the planet to at least one more generation of stagnancy.

She was absolutely forbidden to interfere. And, having to sit helplessly by and watch nothing happen, she had grown so bored she hardly dared think about it.

Now was time for leave, and reassignment. Her "death" had been arranged; her successor had been briefed and was even now aboard the Patrol ship which would land him with utter secrecy to take over his carefully prepared rôle in the local society. . . and she was on her way to Cyclops, a planet she had never conceived she might want to visit.

Yet she had welcomed the reasonless order to come here before proceeding on leave. The delay gave her time to arrive at the decision she had postponed so long: stay on, ask for transfer to some lower-paying job, or resign?

She thought enviously of Gus Langenschmidt, the Patrol Major who had maintained the beat including her assigned world when she first went there; he was aging, greying, even running to fat when she last saw him, yet because he could think of no better purpose to which to devote his accrued longevity, he was continuing far beyond the maximum service-time which qualified for ten-to-one pay. Five centuries was the limit of credit. Fifty years in the Patrol.

More than the total of years I've yet lived, Maddalena reflected. *How is Gus? Where is he? It would have been easier to endure my job if I'd known he was still going to call two or three times a year—but they pulled him off his beat to do something else when he topped the limit, and I could never like his successor so well.*

The communicators announced the imminence of planetfall. The whisper of air began on the hull, like the drumming of scores of marching feet. Maddalena leaned back and closed her eyes, struggling once more with the irresoluble problem. She scarcely noticed the actual landing period, although her fellow passengers were chattering and joking and exchanging snippets of information about Cyclops. A rough world, they thought it was.

Rough world! Maddalena echoed silently. *These soft-handed chair-warmers should go where I've just come from!*

And yet ...

Her mind drifted back two decades on the instant. "A predatory kind of world"—that was the description she had been given when it was first learned Cyclopeans were behind the interference with a ZRP which she had cancelled out by an inspired improvisation.

What did they want her here for, anyway? Why in the galaxy had that message come through at the Corps base where she had been trying to decide whether to go all the way home to Earth for her leave-year, instructing that she be sent to Cyclops on the next available flight?

The answer turned up the moment the locks were opened on the landing-ground—or rather, pontoon. Cyclops, having so much water, had correspondingly little dry ground available for parking spaceships. More than a dozen vessels were in view from the seat in which she still sat listlessly although the others had risen excitedly to await permission to step outside. The gawky shapes of cranes, the abstract formations of hulls in process of cutting up for scrap, the clean bright rails of overhead gantries, wove webs of metal across the blinding blue background of a summer sky.

She had not expected to find such bright light; the primary of the world she had left was cooler than Earth's, but that of Cyclops was whiter and hotter.

A man in summer undress uniform, hair clipped close and indicating that he was called on to fly space where long hair was forbidden because it was dangerous inside a helmet, hauled himself dexterously through the lock even before the mobile gangway trundled into position. He peered down the shadowy aisle of the passenger cabin.

"Senior Lieutenant Santos?" he inquired.

Maddalena stirred and got up.

"The base commandant is waiting for you," the man said. "Would you come with me?"

The other passengers exchanged resentful glances, especially the woman. She had never been out of range of civilised cosmetic treatment, and her age was impossible to assess, whereas Maddalena had had to age the full twenty years she'd spent where cosmetics were mere primitive pastes and powders.

She obeyed the instruction apathetically. But the moment she came to the lock and saw who was waiting below in the open cockpit of the ground-skimmer, she forgot everything in a wave of pure joy.

"*Gus!*" she shouted, and flew down the gangway three steps at a time to hurl her arms around his neck.

"Easy, girl, easy!" he said, disengaging her grip. "I have to maintain some show of authority around this dump, even though I hate it. Let's have a look at you. It's been a long time."

Maddalena pulled back to arm's reach and studied her old friend. "You look better on it than I do," she said with a twinge of envy. And indeed he did; his grey hair had been treated, his face smoothed to wipe away worry-lines, his waistline trimmed to a lean youthfulness. In his immaculate commandant-rank uniform, he looked like a come-on advertisement for Patrol recruitment.

"Have to maintain appearances, the same way you've had to," he grunted. "Here, get in and I'll run you back to my HQ for a bit of refreshment. Your gear will be taken care of. It's not often I get the chance to use my position for my own amusement, but this time I've done it, and you're getting the finest treatment the planet can afford."

"Amusement?" Maddalena said, relaxing with a sigh into the soft padding of the passenger seat. "Did you fetch me here simply for amusement?"

Langenschmidt, easing the ground-skimmer around the tail of the newly-landed ship—the metal shell of the pontoon resonated under them—shot a startled glance at her.

"Weren't you told why you were being sent here? I'd have expected you to raise hell at having your leave postponed when you've waited twenty years for it!"

"No, I just did as I was told." Maddalena narrowed her eyes against the brilliant sunshine and let her gaze rove over the tidily-parked spaceships.

"Hm! You must have changed in the years since we last met," Langenschmidt said. "You used to be a considerable spitfire. Well, I—Well!" He ran his hand around the collar of his full-dress jacket. "I'd better start by explaining, hadn't I? It's to do with the ZRP's, of course. The row about non-interference has blown up yet once more—it's been in the wind since shortly before I was recalled from my beat and put in charge here, and I was put in charge here for precisely the reason that the centre of the whole brewing row was right on Cyclops."

Maddalena, hardly paying attention, made some sort of sound interpretable as an interested comment.

Langenschmidt went on: "In fact, some of it was to do with our little affair at Carrig. Although they were never able to come out and complain openly, the pride of the Cyclops government was badly hurt by the fact that a hundred or so Cyclopeans had been dropped into volcanoes by dirty smelly barbarians, and that we hadn't acted to stop this because of the principle of non-interference with ZRP development. It takes years to stir up trouble when there are two hundred and whatever—two hundred sixty, isn't it?—worlds with a say in running the Corps, but a determined party can get the wheels turning eventually. And on Cyclops we have just such a determined party. Her name is Alura Quist, and if there weren't officially a representative government here I'd say she was a dictator. She's just—ah—unstoppable.

"The Cyclopeans don't like having our base here, but

they can't balance their planetary budget without the revenue it brings in. So short of kicking the Corps off-planet, there's only one way they can get back at us for the Carrig business. That's to attack our prized principle of non-interference. And with a view to this, Quist is right now staging a big conference on the subject, with delegates from all kinds of worlds including Earth, and frankly I'm horrified at the influential names she's managed to rope in.

"The problem is in my lap, Maddalena, and I've worried myself stupid about it. They put me here to try and stave off what Quist is doing, and I'm losing out. When I heard you were at the end of your tour, I thought, 'By Cosmos! She's from Earth, and out this way Earthborn Corpsmen are few and far between—she's served as an on-planet agent, so she has first-hand testimony available.' For all these and several other reasons, I thought maybe you'd jolt my mind out of its old grooves and somehow inspire me to get the better of Quist."

Maddalena stirred and turned her finely-shaped head. Her former look of fragility, Langenschmidt noted, had faded, and she seemed toughened and far less feminine.

"After twenty years watching a gang of Zarathustra refugees getting nowhere, Gus, I'm pretty well convinced myself that it's a crime to leave them to make fools of themselves. I'm sorry to disappoint you within minutes of our first meeting in years, but that's the way I feel right now, and if you want to convince the delegates to this conference that non-interference is the right course, you can start by trying it on me!"

III

For the third time Bracy Dyge began on the miscellaneous collection of transistors littering the bottom of his spares box, hoping against hope that the fault in his fish-finder would put itself right. He was four days from port, even if he started home right away, in this sluggish ancient trawler which represented his whole family's means of support—with himself as sole able-bodied seaman. He had been three days on the fishing-grounds, and only last night had he cottoned on to the fact that the reason for his inability to locate any schools of oilfish lay in an equipment fault, not in a total absence of fish.

For some reason far beyond his rudimentary technical knowledge to fathom, the fish-finder refused to signal anything closer than the bottom of the sea. With maddening precision it delineated on its circular screen the profile of the rocks three hundred feet below his keel, but it wouldn't even show the big plastic bucket he was trailing as a sea-anchor.

Transistors were expensive, and it was impossible to tell by merely looking at them whether they were in functional condition or not. Accordingly, he couldn't say whether those he had salvaged at various times and popped in the spares box were better, or worse, than the ones installed in the fish-finder already. He could merely try every possible combination until he had exhausted the last permutation, and since there were altogether sixteen transistors in the fish-finder and seven in the spares box, it was proving an impossibly long job.

At least, however, it was ridding him of some useless junk. Two of the spares had put the fish-finder completely out of action, and these he had tossed overboard with annoyance.

The sun was baking hot, and the sea was completely featureless. His trawler, shabby and paint-peeling, was the only sign of life as far as he could see. On the afterdeck, in the exiguous shadow of a torn plastic awning, he sat with legs crossed, using the front plate off the fish-finder housing as a tray for the loose parts. He was very lean, and the summer had tanned his naturally-dark skin to the colour of old rich leather. His hair hung around his shoulders in thick braids, and a shiny but sea-tarnished chrome ring was threaded through the pierced lobe of his left ear. Anyone with a knowledge of the culture of Cyclops would have placed him instantly, even without stopping to consider his off-white loincloth and elastic sandals: a fisherboy from one of the sea-hemisphere ports, most likely Gratignol, and doing rather badly this year.

Correct. Morosely, Bracy discovered that another transistor was worthless, and that made three over the side.

At least, he promised himself, he was not going to turn for home before he had exhausted all possibilities for self-help. Even then . . .

His stomach churned and his mind quailed at the prospect of going home with an empty hold. Better, surely, to cruise at random until his nets chanced on something for the family to eat, even if he found no oilfish. Oilfish were the only salable species in this part of the ocean; eating fish could be got by anyone, simply by casting a few lines with bait. Oilfish travelled in vast schools of eight to ten thousand, but because the schools were so big they were likewise concentrated, and without a fish-finder one might hunt for weeks and not cross the path of a single school.

If only he belonged to a different family . . . ! If he were one of the Agmess boys, for instance, six brothers of whom two had sufficient technical skill not merely to do their own electronics repairs but actually to build equipment for other families' boats . . . But by the same token, they guarded their knowledge well. He would have to go home and pay for their assistance, or pay someone else—what with, after a fruitless voyage? Agmess boats had radio, too, and in the event of a breakdown they could signal for help, whereas he was on his own, in charge of the boat which supported his four sisters, his grandmother and his eight-year-old younger brother.

He was himself seventeen years old. He had been the breadwinner of the family since the great storm of the winter before last during which his parents had been drowned in the capsizing of a lifeboat put out to rescue a damned fool.

Add me to the list, Bracy told himself sourly. *My parents would be dreadfully ashamed to see me in this stupid mess!*

He paused in his thankless task and cast a casual glance over the burnished shield of the sea, not expecting to see anything but the water and the sky. His heart gave a lurch and seemed to go out of rhythm for several beats, and he almost spilled the spare parts from the makeshift tray balanced on his legs.

Jackson's buzzards! This far north, they could mean only one thing—a wolfshark!

With frantic haste he gathered the bits of the fish-finder and thrust them in a bag where at least he could find them again, and scrambled to his feet. There was one other way of tracking oilfish besides using electronic aids, and that was to follow a wolfshark as the buzzards did, until its eagerness for prey led it to a school. It could sense the same nutrient-rich currents as all the other fish, and those currents always defined the oilfish's path.

Of course, not all such currents held oilfish—there were too many of them. But it was an idea.

He hesitated, eyes screwed up against the glare, raising the sole of one foot to rub it on the calf of the opposite leg as he always did when concentrating on a problem. There were several factors to weigh before a decision was reached. First off, this wolfshark must be a whopper to have so many buzzards trailing him. Second, he was already four days from home, and a wolfshark finding plenty of prey might kill the clock around for a week before tiring and turning towards the equator again. Third, although he had heard about using a wolfshark as a pilot on the traces of an oilfish school, he had never known anyone really do it—it was needlessly chancy now that everyone sailing from Gratignol could afford a fish-finder.

Finally, if a wolfshark that size decided to attack his trawler, it could probably sink it with a single fierce charge.

Bracy drew a very deep breath. Now was the time for desperate measures, he concluded, and went to see whether he was equipped for the job.

Stores were no problem, apart from water, and unless the weather broke he could keep the solar still going. Power, likewise—during the day he drew enough to move the boat at a sluggish walking pace from silicondynide sails spread to catch the sun, and at night he could spare a little of his stored reserves. He could risk a couple of days on the wolfshark's trail.

Defending himself if the beast turned nasty was another matter altogether. His only weapons were two fish-gaffs, rather corroded from long use and one in particular looking likely to snap soon, and an unreliable self-seeking seine, not much use for anything except bringing up jellyfish to be melted in the sun.

One moment! An inspiration struck him. In the emergency locker he had at least half a dozen signal rockets, which on a sparsely populated world like this needed to reach stratospheric altitude if they were to be any use. They weighed sixty-five pounds apiece, and were triggered automatically by contact with sea-water at one-hour intervals after the life-raft was cast overboard.

He spent fifteen sweaty, swearing minutes manhandling two of them into position on the forward rail, and fishing up a bucket of sea-water to fire them with. If luck and judgement combined, he could give even a monster wolfshark a meal worth remembering with these things.

Then, feeling remarkably cold despite the heat of the day, he fed power to the weakly-responding reaction jets and the trawler began to creep in the wolfshark's general direction.

He was about a mile distant when the skimmer came in sight.

It seemed to appear from nowhere. It was so low in the water, even the shallow troughs of this oily swell had concealed it until it got up on its planes and spewed a frothy plume astern. There seemed to be nothing of it, too—just a platform with a slightly raised rim forward, and a man lying on it, his face masked with a visor against the sun.

Bracy gulped. Going after the wolfshark—? Yes! For he was lying on the butt of a harpoon-gun, and a gleam of sun caught the barbs of the missile.

He saw the wolfshark then, and wished he hadn't come near after all, for it was gigantic beyond his worst nightmares—its span as great as the entire length of his trawler.

The scene of the man on the skimmer confronting the horrible aquatic killer lasted just long enough to burn into his memory, before a sonic boom thundered across the sky and the tableau, one second old, dissolved into a chaos of spray and shrieking cries from the buzzards, which had withdrawn to a safe height after vomiting their half-digested stomach contents.

The skimmer vanished as suddenly as it had appeared, in a whirlpool generated by the passage of the wolf-shark, and a dozen fragments sailed into the air to land at distances up to a hundred feet away. Of the man who had been on it, Bracy saw nothing more for the moment. Chiefly, this was because he was no longer wasting time on looking. He had stopped his engines on solar power and feverishly switched to stored reserves—not that that would enable him to outrun the monster, but at least it would give him a chance to dodge if he timed the manoeuvre correctly.

He waited, wholly tense. Would the beast ignore him, or—? No, his luck was out. For, having turned in a lazy circle, it was rising to the surface again and surveying the upper side of the sea.

This was an old rogue, clearly, as well as a monster. No sooner had it sighted the trawler than it hurled itself forward.

Bracy was yelling at the top of his voice—he had no idea what words he was uttering, but they might have been curses. By crazy guesswork he aligned the trawler on the wolfshark's course, slopped water over the firing mechanism of both rockets, and hurled himself into the well of the deck, hoping the blast would be deflected from him.

One—two—three heartbeats, as widely spaced as measured footfalls, intolerably slow.

And the universe exploded.

Dazed, he picked up his bruised body, feeling as if it belonged to someone else, and put his head over the well's edge to look at the deck. Two of his solar sails were ripped, and the plastic awning which had given him shade had blown clear out of sight; there were char-marks on the planking and the window of the sternhouse was smashed.

But there had been a very satisfactory calamity twenty yards from his bows. He could tell, even before looking over the side, because the buzzards—not choosy about what carrion they ate—had descended already to replace the food wasted in panicky vomiting.

The writhing corpse of the wolfshark, torn almost in two, was pumping its life's blood in great oozing gouts into the ocean.

Limp, Bracy had to cling to the rail—and instantly snatched his hand away. It was still hot from the blaze of the rockets' exhaust. *A miracle I didn't set the ship afire,* he thought wanly.

He looked apathetically at the water. Now he'd lost two solar sails, and his pilot to an oilfish school, for nothing.

He stiffened abruptly. What was that in the water yonder? Something writhing—as though beating at the sky?

The man from the skimmer! Still alive, floating on some buoyant section of his craft—even having the strength to utter faint cries, now that Bracy's ears were attuned to the sound half-masked by the whinnying of the buzzards.

With infinite effort he put the trawler about and drew alongside the floating man. He was by then too weak to help himself; Bracy had to gaff him through a pair of cross-belts on his back. And small wonder he was weak. When he was dragged from the water, he proved to have lost one leg from the knee down to the fangs of the wolfshark.

"Don't—worry," the man whispered, seeing Bracy stare aghast at the injury. "Suit—will stop—the bleeding."

What suit? Bracy peered closer. The man's skin was covered with a transparent film of some kind, that must be it, and it was contracting now of its own accord, forming an automatic tourniquet around the amputated leg so that the flesh turned death-white and the bleeding reduced to a capillary leakage.

Well, that settles it, Bracy thought glumly, and went to fetch another signal rocket, this time to cry for help from wherever it might be available.

IV

Even on a poor world like Cyclops, the Corps enjoyed the best of everything. It was a necessity to compensate personnel for the often heartbreaking tasks that faced them; likewise, however, it was a drawback in the same way as the pay system based on longevity treatment, creating envy and troubling Corps selection boards with mobs of totally unsuitable candidates.

Symptomatic of Corps luxury here was Langenschmidt's home and headquarters, a villa crowning the highest point on the island which the Cyclops government leased to them. There was no need for the commandant to be in close physical touch with his responsibilities in the repair-yard and port—electronic links served the purpose and permitted the privacy preferred by a man whose longest service had been on a lonely Patrol beat one tour of which might take a decade.

His dismay at Maddalena's unexpected response to his first remarks after their meeting kept him silent until they were together in the long, low, cool main room of the villa, with the panorama of the island and its offshore pontoons spread like a map in front of the wall-high windows. Then, cradling a drink in both hands, he leaned back in a contoured chair and stared at this woman whom subconsciously he had still regarded an hour ago as the hot-headed stand-in agent of the Carrig affair, twenty years previous.

He had grown accustomed to the changes wrought in himself by a return to comfort and civilisation—the reversal of the aging effect, for instance. The sight of Maddalena at a "natural" forty-five years of age was a shock to him. Her bones were still fine, her head still as exquisitely shaped as an abstract sculpture, her eyes still bright as gems on either side of her regal nose, sharp as though to symbolise her innate curiosity. But her skin was coarse, her hands were rough, and there was an aura of exhaustion in her attitude and her voice.

To try and dispel the disturbance she had caused in his mind, he said with insincere heartiness, "Well, Maddalena! How have things been going for you since we last met?"

"Badly." She made no move to sip the drink provided for her, although she had taken a dry savoury crackerball from a bowl and was rolling it absently between her fingers. "I doubt if it was more than a logbook entry for you, but you may remember that Headman Cashus was assassinated soon after my assignment, and with him went any hope of progress. So—"

She crumbled the crackerball into dust and dropped the fragments back in the dish. "So I've spent one hell of a long time watching absolutely nothing happen. And you?"

"Ah—I've been learning a new trade and finding I'm not very good at it. Contemporary diplomacy, I guess you'd say. I haven't seen *nothing* happen, but on the galactic scale things take place so slowly as to make a fair approximation." Langenschmidt hesitated. "Maddalena, were you serious in what you said earlier, about non-interference, or was that just due to tiredness after your trip?"

"The tiredness has been building up for a long, long time." Now, finally, she tasted her drink, making no comment on it. "And—yes, I'm serious."

"Are you going clear back to the point of view I had such trouble kicking you out of—along with Pavel Brzeska—when we were going to Carrig?"

"No. That was the preconceived notion of a silly girl. It's been a long time, Gus, even for a Corpsman, and I've—changed, I guess."

"Now look here!" Langenschmidt leaned forward. "You've been on Thirteen, which barely counts as Class A, where the refugees have had extremes of climate to contend with, and in any case started off on the worst possible basis by having no adequately trained leaders. I can understand the sight of a primitive peasant community getting anybody down. But before you change sides on the question of non-interference, think of Fourteen and Carrig—you should see the recent reports from there, incidentally. Think of Seven, where they're developing some new biological and genetic skills, or Eighteen, where there are some language changes going on which will eventually influence the whole pattern of human communication."

"Think of Five," Maddalena countered. "Unless they've licked the cerebral palsy problem, the survivors there are back to grunting like apes."

There was silence for a few minutes. Unhappily, Langenschmidt chewed his lower lip and stared at Maddalena, wondering what next to say.

The problem was a recurrent one, and had been debated for a century and a half. Its roots, though, lay much further back—to be precise, some seven hundred and seventy years before, when the primary of a planet called Zarathustra went nova. For six hundred and thirty years thereafter, it was believed that only a small handful of refugees had escaped—to Baucis Alpha, on the Solward side. Then, without warning, radio signals began to be received from the opposite direction: fruit of generation upon generation of dedicated workers starting from no better level than the salvaged scrap in a single starship, climaxing in the conversion of an asteroid into a huge generating station fed by solar power and oriented to form a bowl-like transmission antenna for messages limping at light-speed back to civilisation.

They came from Lex's Planet, otherwise known as ZRP One: the first Zarathustra Refugee Planet to be located and recontacted. Now, it was part of the galactic union, and regarded as a civilised world.

From there, it had been learned that no fewer than three thousand ships got away from the night side of Zarathustra, and the far quadrant of its orbit, carrying some two and a quarter million people. The Patrol, constituted a couple of centuries before, was given the task of tracking down the remaining survivors, if any.

Twenty-one worlds had now been found where fugitives had landed. On some, they had not only survived, but built up during their period of isolation quite interesting and respectable cultures. Few of them boasted technology to more than rudimentary level, but some had other achievements—such as those Langenschmidt had cited to Maddalena—which promised new avenues for human cultural or scientific development.

After much argument and heart-searching, the non-interference rule was formulated and applied. Unless the ZRP's succeeded in re-contacting civilisation themselves, they were to be left to evolve along the paths they had themselves created. There were many reasons for this. On some planets there had been evolutionary changes due to environment: on all, there had been cultural disruption, and centuries of "natural" breeding, four to five generations per century, had magnified the discontinuity. Perhaps most significant of all, galactic civilisation was slowing down its former progress, as though the distance between the stars imposed a psychological as well as physical barrier on cross-fertilisation of cultures. Seemingly, one felt there was little point in research or inventiveness when for all one could determine on some other of the 260 human planets the same work had already been carried out.

Left to themselves, it was suggested, the ZRP's might rediscover the basic human drives of curiosity and ultimately re-infect the rest of the race.

Elsewhere, there had been a cultural smoothing

process. Worlds like Earth were looked up to, but only the superficialities of fashion spread, not the real changes which underlay them, and consequently things were much the same everywhere as they had been when the Patrol was set up. Backward worlds struggled to catch up to the average standard, and some did so, but the worlds above average were placid and lacked any initiative.

Maddalena stirred in her chair and raised her eyes to her old friend's rejuvenated face. "Who's spearheading the campaign this time? ZRP One as usual, presumably."

Langenschmidt pounced. "No, and that's the most interesting part of it. It used to be fashionable for One to shout about the shocking way their kinfolk were being left to rot instead of rescued and brought home. But this conservative tradition has died out lately, and I think this is because it's taken until now for One to mesh completely with galactic civilisation and discover just how great a change was wrought in their own culture by their isolation period. Now, One's spokesmen are mostly keeping quiet, and we're hoping they will eventually plump for non-interference themselves.

"In their place, we have Cyclops beating the drum, as a result of the Carrig affair in my personal opinion, and a whole lot of charitably-minded but short-sighted people from the older worlds, including and especially Earth. What they fail to understand—I say—is that Earth-type luxury isn't the perfect human way of life. They want to impose it as a standard everywhere, whether or not the recipients enjoy the cultures they have at present, whether or not these cultures are productive, creative ones."

"Thirteen's certainly isn't," Maddalena muttered.

Langenschmidt didn't answer. His eyes had turned towards the window, and widened on seeing a line of brilliant sparks like stitches sewn upward across the blue of the sky.

"Hullo!" he exclaimed. "That's an emergency rocket. Some fisherman in difficulties, presumably. We're always having to nursemaid local folk—either fisherman who go too far to sea with inadequate equipment, or upper-crust playboys out wolfshark-hunting whose nerve fails them at the crucial moment. Still, it interrupts the monotony."

He addressed himself to a communicator panel discreetly blended with the room's no-nonsense decor.

"Anyone taking action on that emergency rocket just now?"

Pause. Then a disembodied voice, sounding irritated, answered him. "Sorry, commandant, what was that?" And, as if re-hearing the question in memory: "Oh! The rocket! Yes, I'll send someone out to gaff the guy and drag him ashore."

"Fine." Langenschmidt's attention reverted to Maddalena. "You know, I think before we finish this argument, I'd better give you a chance to see galactic civilisation, Cyclops-style, so that you can learn all over again what a shallow thing it really is. Take the situation here at present as a shining example. We have this woman Alura Quist, who runs things, as I told you. She's certainly very capable and ruthless. But to have to confine her efforts to Cyclops, which is so poor it still runs on fission rather than fusion, galls her. She doesn't see why Corps personnel should enjoy longevity payments, to start with, when she is aging and having to send clear back to Earth for even her cosmetic treatments. I think in fact some of her hostility to us is due to nothing more abstract than simple jealousy. A woman afraid of losing her youthful looks is a sad case. She has an official lover, one of the handsomest men I've ever seen, who's also a kind of planetary hero, a former spaceman who suffered some kind of crippling injury in creditable circumstances. I don't know the full details. She treats him like a—a tame animal, as it were. Shows him off: here he is, the famous Justin Kolb, and he's my lover. Follow me?"

Maddalena gave a listless nod. She had heard all this, apart from the story of Kolb, at the time of the Carrig affair, when a group of Cyclopean entrepreneurs learned from a failed Corps probationer the location of ZRP Fourteen and its deposits of high-yield radioactives. They had operated a mine with local slave-labour for a considerable time before the Patrol managed to displace them, and Cyclops had smarted ever since under the knowledge that a bunch of ZRP barbarians had dropped civilised men—so-called—down a volcano, the standard punishment for the crimes they had committed by the local ethical yardstick.

"I honestly don't think Quist has any interest in the ZRP's as such," Langenschmidt pursued. "She wants to get back at the Corps for personal reasons of jealousy, and the existence of a fund of hostility due to the episode on Fourteen provides her with a handle. If we were to abandon non-interference for sound, rational reasons, I'd swallow the decision—gagging, maybe, but I'd stomach it. But to do it for such a—"

The disembodied voice spoke again from the communicator. "Commandant?"

"Yes?" Langenschmidt half-turned in his chair.

"That signal rocket. I thought you'd be interested to know about it."

"Not especially, but tell me anyway."

"We've found one of the Gratignol fishermen—a boy, rather, not more than seventeen, they say. He's tangled with a wolfshark being hunted by a—uh—rather notorious person. He fished said notorious person out of the water short of most of one leg. Luckily for him, he was wearing a medisuit, and though he's unconscious he isn't dead. But it's who he is which may interest you."

"Well, then, spit it out," Langenschmidt grunted.

"It's Justin Kolb," said the disembodied voice.

V

Alura Quist was pleased with the way things were going. Not even the reflection which came back to her from the polyview mirror at which she was preparing for the official banquet due at sunset could wholly dispel the mood of grim satisfaction the offworld delegation had generated in her.

Of course, those from the wealthier worlds such as Earth had felt patronising about the best Cyclops could offer, but it was out of keeping with their professed charitable intentions towards the underprivileged of the ZRP's to make open complaint, so they had been on their best behaviour. And the ferocity of the representative from ZRP One—Omar Haust, an old man now but still vehement—outweighed a dozen of his fainter-hearted colleagues. He still clung to views that most people on his planet had reluctantly abandoned.

The banquet would be magnificent; the food and liquor would be so expensive as to have to figure as a special entry in the planetary budget for the year—but never mind, it could appropriately be written off against a one per cent surcharge on the rental of the Corps Galactica base. Afterwards there would have to be speeches, of course—curious how tradition lingered in these formal areas of human activity, even after countless generations—but she could endure that. In sight of a success schemed for over so many years, she could put up with a couple of hours' repetitious mouthing.

"We of Cyclops," she said to the mirror, and watched how the muscles of her throat moved with the words, "are not among the most prosperous peoples of the galaxy. Yet what we have we do not regard selfishly. We would eagerly share it with those who are still worse off than we. In pre-galactic days, the historians tell us, there was a fable recounted about a dog which made its bed on the fodder of a draft-animal and so caused the animal to starve."

She paused, at first because she was still uncertain about including this arcane literary reference even now the speech-compositor had shorn it of obsolete words like "manger" and "ox", and then to carry out yet one more inspection of her appearance.

She was still slender; she had the nervous, energetic constitution which assured her of boniness rather than excess fat in her declining years. Her hair, fair and warmly coloured, was impeccably dressed and framed a strong face in which her eyes were blue and brilliant as sapphires. Her gown was of Earthside manufacture—dated, no doubt, in the eyes of the visitors from the mother world, but suiting her so well she could disregard that minority opinion.

How long would it all last? Her mouth twisted into a harsh grimace, instantly destroying her usual prettiness, as the thought of such a man as Gus Langenschmidt crossed her mind. After fifty years patrolling a beat among the ZRP barbarians, he was promised survival in good health and artificial youth when she was long relegated to footnotes in local history records.

That fact could scarcely be changed. But the purpose to which he had dedicated his life could be emptied of meaning.

Oh, the draft of her speech would do well enough. She let that matter drop, and spoke to the attendant manicuring her toenails on another subject which was currently worrying her.

"Would you tell Justin Kolb that I wish to speak with him before the banquet?"

"Is he going to be there, mistress?" the girl countered.

Quist started. Was there mockery in that level voice?

There was no obvious sign of it in the dark eyes which met hers; she relaxed fractionally.

"What do you mean? Of course he will be there. Why not?"

"I understood from his valet, mistress, that he had not returned half an hour ago."

"Returned?" Bewildered, Quist stared down at the girl. In the past two days, since the arrival of the offworld delegates, she had spared scarcely a moment to think of her lover. She had been vaguely aware that he had gone off somewhere, but had assumed without question that he would be back for tonight's major official function.

She slapped the old-fashioned communicator built into her dressing-table and spoke to the air. "Has Justin Kolb come home yet?"

"I am his valet, mistress," a suave voice replied. "No, he has not yet returned."

"Where is he, then? Has there been a message?"

"No message, mistress. If you wish, I will attempt to contact him."

"Do you know where he is?" Belatedly, it struck Quist as bad for her image not to know already, but she could hardly recall the words once spoken.

"Approximately, mistress. He went wolfshark-hunting at the extreme northern limit of the species' range."

Time seemed to stand still. Finally, her voice ragged, she whispered, "Contact him and find out—find out when he will be back."

And when he does come home, she finished silently, *I'll teach him a lesson he'll never forget for his impudence in disregarding my orders to be here tonight.*

In fact, it might well be time to dispense with Justin Kolb—send him back to the menial job where but for her he would now be slaving out his miserable existence, one leg reduced to a stump by the freezing cold of space.

Cyclops had no slack in its economy to allow for the luxury of unproductive cripples.

She was making alterations to the seating arrangements for the banquet when the communicator sounded again. Was it Justin calling? She closed her eyes for a second, wondering how she could bring herself to get rid of this man whose half-tamed spirit represented the second most constant challenge of her life.

"Mistress, it is I once more," the valet said. "I have bad news, I regret to say."

She could not speak, but waited passively. The girl completed her toe-manicure and gathered her equipment to move away.

"Justin Kolb is in hospital at the Corps Galactica base. He was attacked by the wolfshark he was hunting and a fisherman rescued him. He will live, they say, but—" The valet hesitated.

"Go on," she said in a dead voice. The next of her attendants, charged with fitting her shoes, came and knelt at her feet.

"He has lost his right foot, and the lower part of his leg, to the wolfshark's bite."

Does the madman *want* to be a cripple? The question sped across her mind, and then was replaced by an uncontrollable wave of pity and sympathy. But for tonight's banquet, she would have jumped up that moment and gone to his hospital bed, to hold his hand and croon comfort.

Oh, Justin, Justin! What's the love of danger that you draw your fire from? One day it will kill you, and I shall instantly be made old . . .

Aloud, she spoke with determination. "Put me in touch with him. At once!"

"I will try, mistress," was the doubtful answer, and the communicator went silent.

All thought of the recriminations she was going to level at her lover had evaporated on this news. She could visualise the way he would have brought her his trophy, defiant because he knew it offended her when he courted danger, yet in some ways shy, too—like a boy uncertainly seeking the praise of his first girl. He would have intended to return for the banquet, had the accident not overtaken him, bringing his tribute, and she would have been both angry and delighted, for knowledge that such a man was her lover comforted her.

The communicator spoke once more. "Alura Quist?" it said, and she recognised the voice.

"Commandant Langenschmidt," she said coldly. "I did not ask to speak to you."

"No, but I thought you'd rather speak to me than nobody at all. Justin Kolb won't regain consciousness for some while—at least a couple of hours. He was severely shocked by his experience. But you can have him back tomorrow or the day after, the doctors say."

She tensed. "With his leg restored?"

There was a blank pause. Then Langenschmidt gave a forced chuckle. "Hardly, I'm afraid. Some people seem to have exaggerated ideas of what our medicine can accomplish. Limb-regeneration overnight isn't among our capabilities."

She had expected no other answer, but she had been unable to prevent the words from emerging—they were driven by the savage jealousy she felt towards the Corpsman for his payment in youth and health.

No matter, anyhow. Justin had lost that leg before, and more than simply the foot and lower part—the whole of it, almost all the way to the hip, from space-gangrene.

"Thank you for your courtesy in telling me," she said without warmth. "I'd have appreciated earlier notification, of course."

"It was my belief that you had other things to occupy your mind," Langenschmidt countered mildly.

With a snarl which made her glad communicator links

on Cyclops were restricted to sound without vision, Quist forced herself to maintain calm. She said, "I will have transport sent in the morning, to bring him home. Will that be convenient?"

"I imagine so, but send a doctor as well, of course." Langenschmidt sounded a trifle surprised, as though he had expected an attempt to persuade him that Kolb's leg should be restored at the Corps hospital.

"Of course," Quist echoed, and silenced the communicator.

She waited a second. Then she spoke to it again. "Find me Dr Aleazar Rimerley, and be quick about it!"

Dr Rimerley was enjoying the sunset when the call came. He was among the wealthiest men on Cyclops, and his home consisted of the surface and the heart of an entire island, some mile or so in circumference. His living quarters were built out into the ocean, so that when he chose—as now—he could sit on a higher level and watch the sky, or else he could move down to the seabed and enjoy the vivid panorama of the ocean's summer life.

His chief personal servant brought news of the call. He rubbed his chin in wonder; he had not been intending to get in contact with Quist again just yet, but a further deal was certain once simple cosmetic treatment ceased to stave off time's ravages. Now, therefore, was as good a time as any to talk to her, since she had initiated the conversation.

He smiled automatically even though she could not see him, and said with extreme heartiness, "My dear Alura Quist! What an honour to speak with you after all this time!"

She brushed aside the social formalities and went straight to the point.

"Doctor, I have another job for you. As far as I know, you're the only person on Cyclops capable of tackling it."

"I'll do my best," Rimerley agreed, and repressed a smile that was more sincere than the original one.

"Justin Kolb has lost his leg again. Wolfshark-hunting."

Rimerley blinked. He had expected something altogether different, almost certainly for Quist herself. This request took him aback.

"I'm having him brought to you tomorrow morning. I count on you to do as thorough a job of regeneration as you did the last time."

"Ah—just a moment," Rimerley said uncomfortably. "It's not the sort of job that can be tackled on a few hours' notice, you understand." In the back of his mind he was running calculations: so long to locate material, so long to make the tissue immunologically neutral, so long to get it here. "I doubt whether it would be possible to handle the case in less than two weeks, I'm afraid."

"Two weeks!"

"That's my rough estimate. Of course, I may be—"

"Then I might just as well leave him where he is. He'll be better looked after than in one of our second-rate hospitals."

A warning tremor ran down Rimerley's spine. He said in a voice suddenly fainter than normal, "Ah—where is he, then?"

"In the Corps Galactica hospital. He was taken there after some fisherman rescued him from the water."

Silence.

"Dr Rimerley?" Quist demanded at last, sounding alarmed.

She was not half as alarmed as Rimerley himself. He could barely choke out his answer.

"On—uh—on second thoughts, perhaps it would be better to have him brought here. At once, the sooner the better." He gulped the rest of the drink he had been sipping while he relaxed for the evening. "Yes, certainly not later than tomorrow morning, on any account!"

He was sweating like a river when he cut the connection.

VI

Soraya was working as usual at the waterworks, and having the inevitable argument with Firdausi about marrying him, which he had been urging on her ever since she achieved puberty, when she heard her name being frantically shouted.

She motioned Firdausi to be silent, and peered through the wraiths of steam from the main cauldron, trying to make out who it was. The voice was a child's, but so hoarse with agitation she could not recognise its owner.

The waterworks consisted of three parts. First, there was the dipper which brought water from the natural pool; this was a chain of buckets on two big wooden pulleys, driven by a yorb which seemed quite content to walk around all day in a circle and get an evening reward of food for its trouble. The dipper emptied its water into the main cauldron, under which a hot fire burned all the time, raising sluggishly bursting bubbles in the contents. Although the water seemed perfectly clear and pure when it was raised from the pool, a scum always formed during boiling, and it was in removing this scum with wooden ladles that Soraya and Firdausi were engaged.

Then the water was run off, a little at a time, into the cooling tank, a tapered cylindrical container of heavy stones mortared with natural cement, whence the townsfolk could fetch it in bucketfuls for use at home.

"Can you see who it is?" Soraya demanded.

Firdausi clambered down from the ladder on which they were working, to get below the clouds of steam, and reported. "It looks like the youngest from next door to you—Baby Hakim."

"Oh _no_!" Soraya gulped, and dropped to the ground

with a lithe flexing of her long legs. Firdausi's eyes followed her hungrily. She was by far the most beautiful unmarried girl in the whole town: sloe-eyed, olive-skinned, with long dark hair and supple, graceful limbs. He wished achingly that his parents were not so concerned with mundanities like a dowry and would give him permission to marry her anyway. He was sure she would make an excellent wife . . .

"Hakim baby!" she cried, dropping on her knees and sweeping her arms around the tearful youngster who came charging up to her. "What's wrong?"

Between sobs of exhaustion and terror, the child forced out the news: Soraya's mother had been taken ill yet again.

"You go straight home," Firdausi instructed. "I'll bring Marouz to you there."

She shot him a smile of gratitude and went racing back to the town.

It consisted of two rows of wattle-and-daub houses facing one another, widely spaced, with large vegetable gardens and runs for livestock surrounding them. Tethered yorbs regarded her incuriously as she sped past, feet splashing in puddles left by the overnight rain which the sky threatened to let flood down again at any moment. In the fifth house from the left was her home; she slammed back the crude wooden gate in the fence enclosing its garden, and ran indoors.

Hakim's elder sister, Yana, was bending over the bed on which lay the wheezing form of apparently an old woman. In truth, Soraya's mother was no more than thirty-seven, but in this harsh environment age descended with the swiftness of tropical night.

And yet it was not mere age—endurable, because visited on everyone—which afflicted her. It was something random, and more deadly. There was a name for it: the quakes. But simply to have a name was no help. What was needed was a cure.

Sick with despair, Soraya glanced at Yana. "Has she been like this long?"

"I found her on the floor by the hearth," the other girl answered in low tones. "See, her dress is scorched—it was lucky I chanced to look in, or she might have been burned to death."

Soraya shuddered. "When? Just now?"

"So long ago as it took Hakim to reach you." Yana shrugged. "I sent him at once."

Soraya clutched her mother's hand, feeling the uncontrollable trembling that racked her weak body, and railed mentally against the capriciousness of fate.

"Shall I go for Marouz?" Yana suggested.

"Thank you, but Firdausi was with me at the waterworks, and he has gone already. Not that he'll be any help," Soraya added bitterly.

"You shouldn't talk so. He's the wisest man among us as well as the oldest!" Yana sounded horrified.

"What use is wisdom without practical applications? He can tell us to be dutiful children and loving parents, and we do our best—and my mother who is the kindest of women has the quakes." Soraya put up her hand to wipe away a tear.

"Sssh! He's coming now," Yana murmured, and turned to bow as Marouz dipped his white-bearded head under the low lintel.

"Honour and profit upon this house," the mage said in a single rapid burst, and limped to a chair which Yana brought up beside the bed. "Hmmm! Has your mother drunk unboiled water, Soraya?"

"You think I would let her?" Soraya jumped to her feet, appalled. "I, who work where I do? What do you take me for?"

"Soraya, that's unwise," Firdausi said softly; he had come in just behind Marouz, holding Baby Hakim's chubby hand.

"I don't care!" Tears were gathering in Soraya's eyes

also now. "I don't care! My mother lies sick to death, and all he can think of is that she might have drunk unboiled water! What has water to do with it, anyway? My father tended the waterworks before me, and he'd never have let her do such a thing, and I wouldn't—and *still* she has the quakes! What can water possibly have to do with it?"

Marouz's face went hard as stone. "We are taught by the wisdom of the ancients—" he began.

"And a fat lot of good it does us!" Soraya blazed. But on the last word she collapsed to her knees before him, her shoulders heaving in helpless sobs.

"There, there," Marouz said, giving her an awkward pat on top of the head. "These things are sent to try us, daughter. We do what we can, but we are still far from understanding all life's mysteries. When you grow as old as I—which may you do!—you'll have learned patience with the inescapable."

"I'm sorry," Soraya choked out. "But I love my mother, and she's done so much for me . . . Is there no help you can give?"

"Spiritual comfort I would offer, but I know your mother as a fine, noble-hearted woman in small need of my advice." Marouz waggled his flowing beard regretfully. "The only counsel I can give is to you. And you know what that is, for I've suggested it before."

"I've urged it on her also," Firdausi put in. "And she won't listen."

"Take my mother away from her own home, and send her who knows where?" Soraya exclaimed. "It seems to me so—so heartless!"

"Now, now, my daughter," Marouz soothed. "We all hate necessity, but that's no use. The Receivers of the Sick are good men, full of ancient wisdom and kindly intentions. Is it not better to see your mother in safe keeping than lying here quivering her life away on this narrow hard bed?"

There was silence after that blunt question, until at last Marouz stirred. "Well, I can do no more than I've done," he said, and reached for Yana's arm to get to his feet. "Make your mind up quickly, Soraya—the Receivers are coming to this area in a few days' time, I hear, and they won't be back for months, at least."

He hobbled out, and automatically they threw good wishes after him in the form traditional for very old persons—"May good health attend you to your grave."

Firdausi caught Yana's eye and she took the hint. Crossing the dirt floor to retrieve her young brother, she said in a strained voice, "Well, I have things to see to next door. I guess you'd like to be alone, anyway."

The moment she was out of sight, Firdausi put his arm around Soraya. "Dearest, why do you torture yourself—and your mother—this way?"

She shook off his grip and took the chair Marouz had vacated, to sit gazing down at her mother, fingers driving their nails deep into her palms as though to share her mother's suffering by self-inflicted pain.

"Shall I sell her like a yorb?" she snapped. "You know as I do that but for the payment we'd never have let a single person go from this town to the Receivers! It may be well enough for towns where they don't teach love for one's parents, but it disgusts me."

"Can you do more for her than the Receivers?" Firdausi countered.

"What do they do?" Soraya demanded. "No one will tell me that! What becomes of those committed to their mercies?"

"You should ask Marouz."

"I did, the first time he made this suggestion. And he could only say that he didn't doubt—'didn't doubt'!—that their fate was better than we ignorant folk could offer."

"Wouldn't almost anything be better than this?" Firdausi argued. "Lying helpless among others equally helpless?"

He dropped to his knees, face pleading. "I admire you for your wish to keep your mother with you, believe me! But looking at her, knowing there's nothing we can do—how can you condemn her to it any longer? Look, why don't you ask her views when she's able to talk again?"

Soraya's face was very pale as she murmured, "I did."

"What did she say?" Firdausi pressed.

"That the payment—if the Receivers accept her—would be dowry for me and I could marry you and inherit the house." She formed the words as though each tasted bad in her mouth.

"But in that case—!" Firdausi rocked back on his heels. "If it's her own wish, what holds you back?"

"They might not accept her," Soraya whispered. "They don't take everyone, do they?"

"But it's a chance, don't you see? What chance has she here of any other fate but a lingering, unpleasant death?"

Soraya delayed her answer for long moments. Finally she said, "Firdausi, all you care about is freeing me to marry you. Suppose I say that if—*if*—I take my mother to the Receivers, this does not mean I intend to marry you."

It was Firdausi's turn to hesitate.

"I think," he said slowly, "that the way you're keeping your mother here, suffering needlessly, is likely to make me less eager to have you for my wife."

She flinched as though from a physical blow, and fresh tears gathered in her eyes. Seeing his advantage, Firdausi pressed it.

"There's something almost selfish about it. You've just told me what her own desires are, yet you insist on going against them. If that's not pandering to your own self-esteem, I don't know what is."

She bit down on her lower lip to stop it quivering, and was only able to speak after a further pause. The words came like leaden footfalls.

"Very well. Go to Marouz and find out when the Receivers are due, and where. And I'll try and borrow a wagon and a yorb to take her."

Firdausi's jubilation showed in his face, although his voice was sober enough as he said, "I do really think it's the wisest course."

He turned and went out.

So I'll do it, Soraya thought bitterly. *But I won't marry you or anyone else in this horrible town. If they take her, I'll burn the house and use the pay to go somewhere I can hide from my shame.*

Abruptly she turned to the water-bucket and began to rinse her hands, over and over, as though to remove some clinging invisible foulness.

VII

Maddalena and Langenschmidt ate their evening meal together in the main base restaurant. Under the influence of the nearest approach to civilised luxury she had enjoyed for many years—the Corps base where she had been most recently was as spartan as any of the other outlying stations—Maddalena's mood of exhaustion and apathy faded. The music, food and wine made her expand like a flower to the sun, so that even before she took the course of cosmetic treatment she was due for traces of the impetuous girl Langenschmidt had formerly known began to peek through.

Unfortunately, it was his turn to become distracted and stare for long silent periods into nowhere. It was some while before Maddalena noticed the fact—she had been gossiping about her experiences on ZRP Thirteen—and when she did, she spoke teasingly to him.

"Why, Gus! Is this any way to treat a guest? I thought you'd spent your time here learning all the correct social behaviour!"

"Hm?" He snapped back to the present with a start. "Oh, I'm sorry. There's something bothering me, and I think I just figured out what it has to be. Please excuse me for a few minutes. I have to check on it."

Maddalena stared at him. Suddenly she leaned forward and put her hand on his. "I'm sorry, Gus. I didn't intend to act this way on seeing you for the first time in so many years. You do have problems to handle, and I shouldn't be disregarding them the way I have been."

"No, this is nothing directly to do with you. At least I don't believe it is. Will you excuse me?"

"Is it something I'm not allowed to know about, or may I come with you?"

"Sure, come if you like. I'm not going far. To a communicator first, then to the hospital if my suspicions prove correct."

"Something about this man Justin Kolb?"

"Very much so."

She pushed back her chair and rose.

The network of communicator links knitted the base together as intimately as the nerves in a living body, so that none of the key personnel need ever be out of reach in the rare event of an emergency. Here, Maddalena thought as she studied Langenschmidt's strong profile against the wall of the restaurant communicator booth, emergencies would be even less common than on most Corps bases. He must make a first-class commandant: thorough, patient, farsighted.

But he had been a first-class Patrol Major, too, and would have been equally efficient as an on-planet agent like herself—had stood in as one during the Carrig crisis, and proved that.

She sighed imperceptibly, envying his adaptability and dedication. By comparison she felt herself pliable, weak and self-centred.

The signal indicating access to the base computer memory shone out of the screen in the booth—the Corps was the only regular user of vision circuits on Cyclops apart from the government.

"Justin Kolb, Cyclopean," Langenschmidt said briskly. "Circumstances attending his retirement from the Cyclops space service, please."

The last word tickled Maddalena's fancy. Imagine saying "please" to a machine! But after a second it didn't seem funny—only characteristic of the man who uttered it.

"Select auditory or visual presentation," the machine requested, and he selected sound, thinking it was more convenient for Maddalena, who had to peer into the booth from outside.

The machine spoke dates keyed to an unfamiliar calendar, and continued. "Kolb, Justin. Asteroid mining engineer, spaceman. Second in command of local system mine-ship *Sigma*. Awarded Medal of Cyclops for heroism following accidental destruction of *Sigma* with loss of captain and fifteen crew. Sustained space-gangrene of right leg to mid-thigh, resulting in permanent retirement from space service. More?"

The gently questioning tone of the last word was a marvel of sophisticated engineering, if you thought about it, Maddalena informed herself absently. What was Gus driving at?

"Who was responsible for regenerating his leg?" Langenschmidt demanded.

"No information specific to this question," the machine answered.

"Damn. Uh—what doctor was in charge of his case and supervised his eventual recovery?"

"Dr Aleazar Rimerley," the machine said.

"Thought it might have been," Langenschmidt muttered, and made as though to turn away. He hesitated, and at length voiced another question.

"What facilities exist on Cyclops for the major regeneration of human limbs?"

"The hospital at the Corps Galactica base is fully equipped for limb-regeneration."

"Are there no other facilities for the job here?"

"No information," the machine said after a pause.

"Ve-ery interesting," Langenschmidt said, and shut the communicator off. "Come on!" he added to Maddalena. "We're going down to the hospital. Are you with me so far?"

"His right leg—both times, including today?"

"You're not stupid, are you?" Langenschmidt said affectionately, and put his arm through hers to lead her away.

"I think you're glad to see me in spite of what I said earlier," she murmured when they had gone a short distance.

"Hm? Oh, of course I am!"

"You *have* learned the socially correct things here!" she snapped, and withdrew her arm.

He seemed still to be puzzling over that crack when they reached the hospital and were shown into the presence of a tall, brown-bearded man in self-sterilising whites, passing time with a chess problem.

"This is Dr Anstey Nole, our senior medical officer," Langenschmidt told Maddalena in passing. "Doc! It's about this Justin Kolb. How is he?"

"As well as you'd expect, seeing he's lost half his right calf and the foot, endured a medisuit tourniquet for long enough to starve the tissues of blood, and been frightened nearly out of his wits by that wolfshark. Not to mention almost being blown to pieces when this fisher-kid let go his rockets."

"What? I saw one of the rockets go up myself—seemed to work perfectly." Langenschmidt blinked.

"Oh, not the one he used to call for help. Didn't they tell you how he dealt with the wolfshark? Set up two of these damned great fireworks on the foredeck of his trawler and let them go pointblank. Tore the wolfshark to ribbons, I gather. Quite a bright kid, I can tell you. He's in here too, being treated for malnutrition, incipient lupus and minor burns sustained when he let the rockets go. Lost half his hair."

"Lupus?" Maddalena put in inquiringly.

"Strictly that's incorrect, I grant you, but it's the term we apply. A skin disease common among the fisher-folk—they get it from overexposure to sunlight and the irritants secreted by oilfish scales. Life on a backward world like this is a pretty unpleasant business sometimes.

Sorry to have brought the subject up." Nole looked uncomfortable.

"You don't have to tell me," Maddalena snapped. "I just completed a twenty-year tour on a ZRP."

Nole looked still more uncomfortable and changed the subject hastily.

"Matter of fact, as soon as he recovers I mean to send this kid to see you, commandant. His name's Bracy Dyge, by the way. Says he wants to be considered for Corps membership. I laughed at him at first, frankly. Then I thought it over, and finally decided: hell, he has initiative, anyway!"

"Every waterfront on the planet is swarming with kids who think they want to join the Corps," Langenschmidt said cynically. "I'm surprised at you, doc. It's the pay they're after."

"He doesn't know about the pay," the doctor said. "At least, I don't think he can."

"What? Of course he must! Everybody—"

Nole interrupted firmly. "No, all the time we were talking it was never mentioned. He just wants to be able to support his family—parents are both dead—some better way than by chasing oilfish. His fish-finder has been out of order, and . . . I asked for it to be seen to in our workshops, by the way. Hope you've no objection. It seemed like the least we—"

"Hell, I didn't come down here to talk about this—this Bracy Dyge!" exclaimed Langenschmidt. "I came to talk about Kolb. In particular, about Kolb's leg."

Nole shrugged. "I've told you all I can, I guess."

"Wrong. You haven't started. You didn't even mention that he'd lost it before."

It was Nole's turn to be astonished, "Nobody told me so! Are you sure about that? Why, it *looked* like a natural leg—what was left of it—when I examined him earlier."

"You wouldn't expect it to look like a false one, would you? Does the name of Dr Aleazar Rimerley mean anything to you?"

"No, I don't believe so. A local sawbones, perhaps?"

"You could call him that. The most successful doctor on Cyclops—has been retained by Quist at least once. Would he be able to regenerate Kolb's leg?"

Nole pursed his lips and looked dubious. "Just possibly. Regeneration of a leg—ah—yes, with half a megabrain computer capacity you could do a fair job from the knee down. It is conceivable, but I didn't realise Cyclops could afford medical computers on this scale."

"This wasn't for a knee-down job. This was from mid-thigh."

"Then I don't believe it," Nole said. "You'd need a full megabrain, and at that the job might not come off." He gave Maddalena an apologetic glance, as though fearing this was distasteful to her. "It's the joint, you see—especially the synovial membranes. Very tricky to programme well."

"What are you standing there for?" Langenschmidt inquired sweetly. "Has, or has not, Justin Kolb two functioning knees?"

Nole made a wordless noise and spun on his heel.

Maddalena sat down on the corner of the table where Nole had set out his chessboard, and stared at Langenschmidt.

"I don't quite see the significance of this," she ventured. "There are places where regeneration is available, and if this man Kolb is the—uh—accepted lover of Alura Quist, could she not have pulled strings to have him treated on some more advanced planet?"

"If she had done so, the memory bank would have mentioned it." Langenschmidt began to pace the room. "I didn't. It gave me an unequivocal answer when I asked who was responsible for Kolb's eventual recovery—it named a Cyclopean doctor, who's probably very good in his limited sphere, but simply hasn't got access to the medical computer capacity needed for regeneration."

Maddalena paled. "But what alternative treatment could he have offered? Kolb did regain his leg, didn't he? Nole might have overlooked the fact that the limb wasn't an original, but he couldn't have overlooked a prosthetic!"

"Exactly," Langenschmidt muttered, and fell silent.

They waited, neither saying anything, for twenty minutes before Nole returned, his face pale above his full brown beard.

"I don't know what put you onto this, commandant," he began, "and equally I don't know how I came to miss—"

"Save the apologies. What have you found now you have looked?"

"His right leg isn't his own. It's not regenerated is what I mean—regeneration counts as own-tissue substance." Nole combed his beard with agitated fingers. "That leaves one possibility. It's a graft. An exceptionally good one, what's more—it must have been selected most carefully to make a pair with the left leg. Well, of course, the moment I discovered this I took a cell-sample and processed it for genetic structure, and I've come up with the most alarming result."

Langenschmidt's face was quite calm, as though he had already worked out what revelation Nole had brought them. He said merely, "Go on."

"Well, it's hard to be absolutely certain, but I'd say on the basis of what I've just seen that the leg's not merely not his own—it's also not Cyclopean in origin. At any rate, the particular gene-structure of the cells I processed has never been recorded on Cyclops."

"Can you tell me where it is from?" Langenschmidt snapped.

"I've set the computers to search, but there may not be a definite reading." Nole combed his beard again. "Commandant, this is the most extraordinary thing I ever heard of!"

VIII

The screen of the subspace communicator lit. The venture was a profitable one; the partners in it had become able to allow themselves such refinements as interstellar vision circuits. It showed a man with a face as cruelly beaked as a Jackson's buzzard, clad in the decent black robe of a Receiver of the Sick, with the hood thrown back on his shoulders. His hair was greying but still luxuriant, and his face was lined more by reflected concentration than by the passage of time.

This was Lors Heimdall, on whom Rimerley was totally dependent.

"What is it?" he grunted, eyes scanning the image of the doctor confronting him. Vaguely in the background could be seen the interior of his headquarters, with a rack of robes hanging like dead bats on the wall, a videograph playing over a recording of some music-drama or other.

If he can't read the crisis straight off my face, Rimerley thought, *I must be over the worst of the shock.*

Indeed, he felt considerably better than he had done when he finished speaking to Quist. As well as taking another stiff drink, he had given himself a shot of mixed tranquillisers and mind-keeners, a blend which he usually only relied on when making the preparations for a major operation. But this affair, of course, might turn out to be a major operation in its own way . . .

"Two things," he said crisply. "Sorry to disturb you, by the way, but you'll see the urgency when I tell you the background. Did I interrupt anything?"

"No, it's early morning here, half an hour past dawn. We weren't ready to move off yet." Heimdall was doubtless impatient, but his tone was superficially affable.

"Where are you at present?"

"Working south from Idiot's Head towards Encampment Hills. Am I to take it you have a special order for us?"

Rimerley nodded. "A double. First off, how would you like to do a favour for Justin Kolb?"

"Another?" Heimdall said acidly. "The bastard has had too many breaks in life already. True, but for his incompetence I wouldn't be where I am now—but I've settled that score, and I'd rather not know. Cosmos, he wasn't even a moderately capable spaceman—just a hothead with a specious brand of charm—and they made him a hero. Or rather, Quist did." He scowled. "Okay. What sort of a favour?"

Rimerley had to wipe away a trace of itching sweat. "Hot here—full summer," he muttered in explanation to Heimdall. "Well, as a matter of fact he's lost his leg again. To a wolfshark this time. The same leg."

"And Quist no doubt wants her tame monkey cured," Heimdall agreed briskly. "Also we must fill the order quickly to keep her sweet against the day when she becomes our biggest client. We have the specifications on record, so it should be fairly easy. Yes?"

"Not altogether," Rimerley muttered. "I mean, that part of it is. But what's resulted from his encounter with the wolfshark isn't so cheerful. He was rescued by some ignorant fisherman and taken to the Corps Galactica hospital—it was the nearest point from which help could get to him, I suppose."

Heimdall's face darkened like the sky before a thunderstorm. "In that case, we're leaving here at once! I want to be on some good and distant planet before the pan boils over, with a change of name and a change of identitraces!"

"Wait!" Rimerley instructed in a soothing tone. "All is not lost, you know. I told Quist to get her boyfriend out of there tomorrow morning at the latest, and bring him to me. There's an excellent chance they won't be interested enough in Cyclopean scandal to know Kolb's history—there's little contact between the Corps and the Cyclopeans, as you're well aware."

"Any at all is too much for me," Heimdall scowled. "How about the genetic pattern of the graft, though?"

"Why should it occur to them to check it?" Rimerley countered. "If they don't know Kolb's story, they'll assume it's his original leg—the match was eye-perfect, remember. Didn't I give you hell finding the exact match, and reject who knows how many faulty samples first?"

Heimdall nodded, but looked worried even so. Rimerley plunged on.

"Even if they do know his story, they'll most likely take it for a regenerated limb. After all, if he's Quist's lover, who would be more likely to afford the journey offworld to somewhere he could find that standard of medical computation? The only thing which would make them stumble on the unmatched genetic pattern would be if they attempted a fresh regeneration themselves, and cross-checked to the left leg."

"Might they not do that?" Heimdall suggested. "It's an open secret that Quist has no love for them, and would discontinue their lease on the island they use if she could. It might occur to them to fix up Kolb to sweeten her a little. A sort of bribe."

"If that were their intention," Rimerley said with exaggerated confidence, "she wouldn't have offered, of her own accord, to have him brought here tomorrow morning, would she? She'd never have bothered to get in touch with me at all, in fact."

"No, I guess that figures," conceded Heimdall.

"And besides," Rimerley pursued, leaning closer to the screen, "we are the ones who are going to offer Quist a bribe. A bribe she couldn't possibly refuse, even if the price were something very helpful to us, like—let's say—

ordering the Corps to abandon their base on Cyclops with immediate effect. That should give them enough to occupy their minds without worrying about Justin Kolb's leg!"

A spark gleamed in Heimdall's eyes. He said, "If you can pull a trick like that to divert the storm, you're cleverer than I thought you were. How will you organise it?"

"Like this," Rimerley said, and began to explain.

The banquet had passed tolerably swiftly, but the speeches afterwards were dragging on to all eternity. Alura Quist had given up listening to the actual words a quarter-hour earlier, and was lost in a maze of private contemplation.

Every now and again her eyes strayed to the seat on her left, occupied by the senior representative of the participants from Earth, which should have been Justin's tonight.

I feel horribly old, she told herself. *And if anyone cares to peer closely enough at me, more than likely I look old. And when I die, what will stand to my memory other than a weatherworn gravestone and some dates in my career which no one off Cyclops will learn in school?*

Even the long-schemed-for plan to overset the Corps's prized principle of non-interference with ZRP's was sour to the taste now, as she contemplated the old man at her right: Omar Haust, from ZRP One, honoured by being seated next to her because he was the only person present whose ancestors had had to endure the mud-grubbing existence of a refugee planet.

And he was disgracing himself.

He had drunk too much, to start with. At the commencement of the evening he had looked ascetic, almost saintly, with his fierce white moustache fringing his upper lip, his halo-like white hair circling his shiny bald pate. But he had continued to drink heavily; for the later courses, he had insisted on waving aside cutlery and eating with his fingers, as a sort of gesture of solidarity with those on the ZRP's who were denied any other implements. Twice his hand, made greasy with the food, let fall full goblets of liquor that splashed all over his seat-neighbours—including Quist, whose prized Earth-made gown was spattered with dark stains. And for the past several minutes, during the speech by the senior Earth delegate, he had been muttering insulting remarks in his own mother-tongue, a divergent offshoot of the common Galactic language which was still sufficiently close for Quist to have flinched at what she half-understood.

Since letting herself drift off into her private worries, however, she had paid no more attention.

Suddenly she was snatched out of a mingled kaleidoscope of self-pity and optimism, in which Justin Kolb figured very frequently, to realise that the old man's patience was at an end. He was on his feet, hammering with the base of his goblet on the table, and every blow splashed fresh gouts of liquor far and wide. The delegate delivering the current speech broke off in horror as Haust bellowed in his thick accent.

"It makes me sick! It makes me want to vomit! Here's all this fine talk about our poor miserable brothers and sisters out on the refugee planets, which we're forbidden to liberate and bring back to the fold of civilisation—and who's spewing out these platitudes? Hm? Who's mouthing these pious nothings about what we ought to do?"

Aghast, the assembled company of notables looked elsewhere for some less embarrassing spectacle than the aged drunkard, slobbering down his chin.

"I'll tell you!" he roared. "A gang of dirty lying hypocrites! That's what you all are! Look at you!" He hurled his goblet in the general direction of the speaker from Earth, a mild-mannered woman of ninety or a hundred with a distinguished political record on her home world; fortunately the missile sailed wide of her.

"Look at you!" Haust repeated. "With the rolls of Earthside fat wobbling around your middle! And all the rest of you, the same. As for *you*—"

He rounded on Quist, who shrank back in her chair. Alarmed attendants moved close, uncertain whether to try and restrain Haust or wait till he actually struck their mistress. She was frozen and could offer them no clue for guidance.

"You're as bad as the rest!" the old man raved. "Who keeps the ZRP's in subju—subju'ation? The Corps stinking Galactica, that's who, and their whining lackeys in the Patrol! And who leases a base right here on Cyclosh—Shyclops—right on this filthy world whatever its name is!—to the triply damned Corps? Why, *you* do! Aargh! Give me some more drink to wash away the taste of you!"

H snatched at the nearest goblet, which happened to be Quist's own, and as he made to raise it to his lips lost his precarious grip on stability and went crashing to the floor.

"I am sure," said the next speaker, "we ought to learn a lesson from what too many of us took simply as a disgusting exhibition." He was a lean man from the twin worlds of Alpha and Beta Lobulae, which having been blessed with few internal troubles had much surplus energy for meddling in those of other systems. "It should have reminded us all that we are not dealing with abstracts, but with human beings, with a capacity to suffer, and suffer more greatly than we fortunate children of happier worlds can know. Indeed, it comes as no great surprise to me to realise that Omar Haust feels himself unnecessarily mocked by the presence of the Corps Galactica base on this planet—whose hospitality and whose government's sympathy with our aims I do not question, but whose action in this respect perhaps casts doubt in the minds of waverers about our ultimate determination."

That, Quist realised with a sinking heart, called for a reply. And it would be useless to state the truth—that but for the income the leasing of that island to the Corps brought to Cyclops, the delegates would not be here; the revenue tipped the balance between Cyclops affording and not affording an interstellar fleet, small though it had to be.

She rose and looked around. She could use the opening of her original speech, she decided, and began on it. The compositor had worked well, and it soon had the delegates listening in calm self-approval, bar the man from Lobulae.

To him, finally, she said with an air of desperation, "It must of course be recalled that in the days when the agreement between my—*our* government and the Corps was reached, the first of the ZRP's had not yet been chanced upon. Far be it from me to decry the useful work the Corps has done, in its capacity as the interstellar counterpart to a police force. It seems only to be in the area of framing policy that they have exceeded their intended brief."

Nods to that.

"However, we are grateful for the suggestion. I'll have the proposal investigated, and if on balance it does appear that such an action would be an effective lever in securing our aims against the opposition of the Corps, I will make a formal statement to that effect."

Applause. She sat down, wishing with all her heart that Justin were here to shower his praise on her, forced though she knew it to be.

Heaven help Cyclops if I have to act on that vaporous promise, she thought grimly, and turned to smile at those delegates who were complimenting her on what she had said.

IX

Nole had gone off again, still in a state of agitation, to see whether there was a print-out from the computer which he had set to tracking the gene-type of the tissue in Kolb's leg-graft.

It was very quiet in the office where Maddalena and Langenschmidt waited for news. The hospital hummed with the same soft efficient noise as an advanced automatic factory; since its business was the repair and maintenance of what were after all the highly complex mechanisms of human flesh, that wasn't surprising. Dimly from beyond the walls noise of other repair work reached them: clashing as hull-plates were fitted to ships undergoing overhaul, the subtly disturbing moan of drive units on test.

Maddalena had been staring at tonight's half moon—small, and reduced in size still further by its distance from Cyclops—for some minutes before she spoke again.

"There are an awful lot of things I can't get clear about the situation here, Gus. Maybe you'd better educate me."

"Hm?" Langenschmidt jerked his head. "Oh! Oh yes. I'm sorry—I'm still working on the false assumption that you were briefed before you were sent to Cyclops. Since you weren't, presumably you know practically nothing about it. After all, it's never been a world to hit the galactic headlines."

"The last time I paid it any attention was twenty years back. There must have been many changes since then."

"Yes and no." Langenschmidt had been perching on the end of the room's single large table; now he grew uncomfortable and moved to a contoured chair, dropping his body into it absently and letting it slump.

"The—the mood of Cyclops, the planetary average of human attitudes, so to speak, is constant over a long period, as it is anywhere. What was the word I heard you apply?"

"Predatory?"

"Exactly. Ummmm . . . Where the hell ought I to start?" Langenschmidt rubbed his face tiredly. "Clear back at the beginning, I guess. It must start with the fact that it's an unsupervised foundation."

Maddalena started. "*Is* is now? That accounts for a great deal, I imagine."

"I'm sure it does. Of the two hundred and sixty civilised worlds, over two hundred followed the standard official pattern—exploration, selected colonisation under the direction of a polymath trained intensively for the development of one and only one particular planet, and eventually opening to immigration. Cyclops is among the anomalous fifty-odd. It's a second-stage offshoot from Dagon. Ring any bells?"

"Of course it does." Maddalena hesitated, then gave a little nervous laugh. "Dear Gus! How little you've changed! You still have exactly the same lecturing manner as you did when you first briefed me on ZRP Fourteen—touchy, expecting this conceited Earthgirl to have ignorance of unplumbable depth."

"I'm sorry." Langenschmidt gave a crooked smile. "So we take the rest as read. They made one of their rare mistakes on Dagon, and picked for its polymath a man who couldn't stand the strain. He clashed with one of his continental managers, who finally couldn't endure it any more and decided he could do better by himself on some other planet. He, and about four thousand followers, left Dagon and set out to—well, to homestead Cyclops, I guess.

"It was as tough in the early days as it must have been on ZRP One, or some other comparatively hospitable ZRP. Naturally, since he'd attracted his followers on the basis of liberty from the authoritarian whims of a bad polymath, the original leader insisted on at least the structure of a representative government, and that's survived, but only as a formality to the degree required to qualify Cyclops as a member of galactic civilisation. Their laws follow the Unified Galactic Code, too. In theory.

"In fact, starting off with so great a handicap, they let all this remain a formality and proceeded to develop a hand-to-mouth pattern they've never escaped from. It's one of the few civilised planets where ruthlessness brings power. Quist, who has been the *de facto* head of government for a long time now, has no better qualifications for the job than sheer love of authority. She enjoys giving orders and having them obeyed that significant one per cent more than anyone else.

"If you want handy comparisons—well, they have to be pre-Galactic. First century atomic era. Earthside areas like Spain, some countries of Latin America, and some of South Asia. Where you had an economy too impoverished to support the governmental structure of a financially efficient administration, but a sort of crust of great wealth overlying it. Half the population are at the poverty line, a third are illiterate, a quarter are diseased—but perhaps one in twenty have achieved some kind of personal success by pure doggedness."

"I didn't realise you knew Earthside history as well as that," Maddalena said after a moment's silence.

"I don't, really, I just needed some guide to Cyclops when they posted me here, and these are the examples our social psychologists dredged up for me."

"What does support the Cyclopean economy? And what's the total population now?"

"Efficient census-taking is one of the expensive luxuries they don't enjoy, but our best estimates are around seven to eight hundred million. Mark you, life expectancy is low; one child in eight dies in its first year. As to the economy: it's self-supporting in respect of food and housing—the climate in the equatorial belt is an advantage there, with very mild rainy seasons and no real winters—and several other basics like textiles . . . It's a safe Class A planet, or the original settlers would never have survived.

"About the only exports are fish-oil, which serves as a source of proteins for further synthesis and ultimate use as a diet-supplement on some nearby vitamin-poor worlds, and raw materials from the asteroid belt. There are some lumps of ore pure enough to be worth shipping long distances. But the margin is slender, and two invisible exports make the crucial difference between getting by and relapsing to starvation.

"One of them is a small tramp space-fleet, consisting of a hundred-odd interstellar vessels. And the other is—all this." Langenschmidt gestured to embrace their surroundings. "Cyclops is conveniently sited with respect to the forward bases in this sector, and we've rented this island since shortly after the Corps was constituted.

"Trapped in their economic snare, the Cyclopeans don't like having us here. Isn't it a truly ancient platitude that the poor don't like the police? But here we are, and they can't afford to be rid of us."

The office communicator sounded, and Nole's voice, nervous, addressed them. "Commandant, can you come down to the computing room? I'm getting results I can't make sense of, and I think you'll want to see them."

"Coming!" Langenschmidt said briskly, and rose.

Very cautiously, Bracy Dyge swung his legs over the side of the bed. It was further to the floor than he had expected. Anyway, this hardly fitted his concept of a bed—it was an elaborate therapeutic installation with a disturbing aura of near-sentience about it, and he would much rather have been on the pile of inflated fish-skins which he was used to at home, three inches from the ground.

He had been instructed to lie here and sleep, but he'd been unable to. After a short lifetime on the edge of starvation, the nutrient and restorative shots he had been given had acted like a violent stimulant—something the doctors should have made allowances for, but hadn't, being used to scaling their treatment to the healthier and better-fed patients they normally had.

He felt, in short, fighting fit. The burns he had suffered when he let off his signal rockets against the wolf-shark had been dressed with something to relieve the pain, and although he had lost half his braided hair and several square inches of skin, the injured area was cool and perfectly comfortable. Nothing distracted him from what was uppermost in his mind—to wit, the fact that he had been brought to half-legendary Corps Island, from which the local inhabitants were strictly excluded.

Tomorrow he would have to ask to be sent away—he owed it to his family to get back to sea and try and complete his unfinished business. He had ventured to tell the doctor of his dream-ambition—being allowed to join the Corps—but something in the answering laugh had convinced him it was a ridiculous proposal. They had promised to mend his fish-finder, and he would have to be content with that as his reward for rescuing the wolf-shark-hunter.

If only it had been one of the men from the Corps base . . . ! But it was useless to wish that the past were different.

Maybe he could beg replacements for his torn solar sails, too. Even so, tomorrow he would have to leave—and lying wakeful without using this opportunity to see how the Corps lived was more than he could endure.

He stole to the door and fumbled with the latch. It proved to be simple in operation, and after pressure on a raised patch in its centre the panel slid back into the wall, revealing an empty corridor beyond.

After cautious listening for footsteps or hushing wheels such as he had heard earlier, when he was being brought in, he darted down the passage and around the first corner.

Here the nature of his surroundings changed completely. Instead of barely delineated doors, there were large oblong windows, and not giving on to the outside, either, like any windows he had seen before. They revealed the interior of the adjacent rooms.

He crept to the first one and peered through. All he could see was a tangle of equipment like the interior of his fish-finder, but much more complicated. He tried to discern its function, and failed; then it moved of its own accord, some shining arm making a connection, and alarmed at this he moved on.

Here what he found was far more interesting. There was a naked woman.

She was tall, and very beautiful even though her skin was darker than Bracy's own—a sign, according to his standards, that she was of his own low class, too poor to sit in the shade when the sun was hot. She lay supine on a padded trolley, eyes closed. Around her, the whole room was filled with mechanisms that moved slowly, slowly, on incomprehensible tasks.

His eyes traced the curves of her shapely body: left arm here, folded over her breast, right arm—where?

With sudden shock he realised that her right arm was in the maw of one of the machines, which was moving up it in precisely the same way as a suckermouth lamprey engulfed its unfortunate prey.

Like all poverty-line children on Cyclops, he had been threatened with the vengeance of the Corps when he misbehaved as a youngster. To see what he mistook for some terrible torture unnerved him, and he uttered a cry of terror.

"What was that?" a voice said, distant but distinct, and he realised abruptly that had he not been so fascinated by what he had discovered he would have heard footsteps approaching. Gasping, he spun, and caught sight of a man and a woman at the intersection of corridors behind him.

"Who in the—?" the man said. "Hey, you!"

Bracy took to his heels, fleeing randomly down the blank-walled passages. Behind him came the fearful pursuers, shouting, until the superior speed which terror lent enabled him to outstrip them, and he came to a dark tunnel-like tube down which he dived, thinking to find sanctuary.

"That must be the fisherboy who rescued Kolb," Langenschmidt told Maddalena. "No one else with hair like that would be in the hospital. And where the hell he's managed to disappear to, *I* don't know. But one thing's sure—he was heading for master operations control, and we've got to winkle him out before he breaks something. See a communicator anywhere? Whatever Nole has found it will just have to wait."

X

Overnight rain had made the track into a muddy swamp. The patient, immensely strong yorb floundered many times, its broad pads sliding on the greasy ground as it strove to drag the laden cart past a particularly treacherous patch. On each occasion, however, Firdausi got down without complaint to break branches from the surrounding undergrowth and spread them in front of the wheels.

The reins limp and slippery in her hands, Soraya found herself stirred to dim gratitude for the boy's silence. Almost, she was minded to go back on her decision that if the Receivers of the Sick accepted her mother she would leave home forever. Perhaps Firdausi did indeed have her best interests at heart . . .

The old woman lay uncomplaining on the heap of soft skins with which they had padded the crude wooden cart. Occasionally her hands twitched in her sleep. It was better that she should sleep, Soraya thought. Even though she had had a long lucid period since her near-fatal attack of the quakes, the disease had weakened her dreadfully; she could hardly walk more than a dozen steps without a fit of fainting, and her skin was shrunken over her wasted flesh.

She had said she was pleased at Soraya's decision to try and get her taken by the Receivers, declaring she had been a useless burden for far too long. But was that a rational opinion, or the apathetic consequence of the debilitating sickness? After so many bouts of it, anyone might wish to get things over and done with.

"Not far now," Firdausi whispered. "One more hill, and we shall be on a good dry road for the rest of the trip."

She gave a nod, but in reality scarcely heard what he had said.

The sky was grey above; the trees around, draped with their curious hair-like foliage, were grey-green and still dripping from the last downpour before dawn. It was a setting which exactly matched her depressed mood.

Suppose they don't take her after all? Suppose they say I've delayed too long—that if I'd brought her to them a month sooner, they could have helped her, but now it's useless? I shall never forgive myself. Never!

The yorb drew the cart over the crest of the last hill before their destination, and as Firdausi had promised they found themselves on a good hard road, well beaten down and with a top dressing of compacted gravel. Ahead, the town loomed, much larger than the village where she had spent her life: there must be almost a thousand houses, she told herself.

It was hard to credit the stories of the ancients—that men had once been numbered in millions, and dwelt among the shining stars . . .

A little distance further on, they encountered a farm labourer backing a balky yorb into the shafts of a cart piled high with edible roots, and he greeted them civilly. When they explained the purpose of their errand, he pointed towards the town.

"The Receivers aren't yet here, but they're expected hourly, I believe. Good health attends my family, luckily, so I made no special inquiry this time. Go to the market square—you'll find others gathered who are afflicted as you are."

"Many thanks," Firdausi said, and urged their yorb onward.

Lors Heimdall's lip curled with utter contempt as the first sign reached him that they were nearing the goal: the smell.

The stupidity of these people! The dirt, the disease, the lack of hygiene! How could they be regarded as human at all when they lived like wild beasts? If this were truly man's "natural state", from which only a slow process of technical evolution had lifted him towards the clean bright cities of galactic civilisation, it was a wonder any progress was ever achieved.

They seemed to lack all rational system, operating by a bunch of crude uncomprehended near-superstitions: boiling their drinking-water, for example—from here, it was possible to see the plume of steam ascending over the local waterworks. That was presumably a *diktat* imposed by one of the original refugees who had kept his head in the aftermath of disaster, and would have made sense in the context of a proper sanitary code. As it stood, it was a pointless ritual negated by the lack of decent drainage.

Still, some of the accidents of cultural evolution had turned out to be advantageous: the institution of the Receivers of the Sick, for instance. That must have begun as a form of quarantine and isolation for sufferers from diseases which the rudimentary facilities of the refugees could not cope with; it would have been hoped that some at least of the patients might recover naturally, but as a precaution they were removed from their own communities to special locations.

The system had fallen almost completely into disuse, because the staff of these quarantine areas were themselves successively wiped out by infections caught from those they were trying to help. But reviving it had provided Heimdall and his men with an excellent cover for their work.

And if it ever came to light what had been done here, there was little chance of swift retribution. Most civilised planets recognised the right of euthanasia for the incurably sick, and provided the debate about non-interference, yes or no, could be kept on the boil the Corps would never dare execute summary punishment.

He found these reflections comforting to some degree—and he needed comfort. For all his mask of dedicated ruthlessness, Heimdall was capable of anxiety, and what Rimerley had told him had been alarming, to say the least.

It was to be hoped that his ingenious trick to provide the Corps with another major headache and distract their interest would work.

His train of attendants—riding yorbs, as he was: no other transportation was known here apart from rough carts—followed him down the hill road towards the town. Behind came the wagon, covered with an opaque cloth screen on wooden poles, in which were the well-guarded secrets of their job. A party of local notables waited to greet them at the town's edge, and after a suitably grave exchange of good wishes they all proceeded together to the market square.

We shall have to do some more propaganda here, Heimdall advised himself as he scanned the horrible collection of palsied and maimed and sickly candidates for the good offices of the Receivers. *We must get it through their heads that an aged crone, or an ill-nourished infant, is beyond hope—what we can "offer to help" is typically a healthy but injured late adolescent.*

Suddenly, as he was about to turn away, he saw the girl sitting with her boy-friend on the last-arrived cart at the side of the square. His heart gave an uncharacteristic leap. To a first glance, it appeared that what he had been asked by Rimerley to locate had turned up without his even looking. Of course, it would require closer examination to make sure, but the chance was so good he found himself grinning in a fashion quite unsuited to his pose in this society.

Nervously, Soraya waited as the Receivers made their

rounds of the sick. Firdausi wanted to hold her hand while they watched, but she could not bear anyone's touch except her mother's. The old woman was awake and kept trying to lift her head, but failed.

At last the Receivers came to their cart, and after acknowledging good wishes peered down solemnly at the wasted body on the heap of skins.

"Your mother?" the leader of the Receivers inquired of them.

"Mine," Soraya said. "Uh—this young man is a friend who came with us."

"I see." The Receiver nodded. He had a face of such sternness—nose cruelly beaked, mouth thin and straight—that Soraya found it hard to recall what Marouz had told her: that these were good men, full of ancient wisdom and kind intentions.

"Come with me, please," he said abruptly, and gestured Soraya to descend from the cart. Shivering a little, she complied, and was astonished when the Receiver set off at a brisk pace towards his own wagon.

Following, she tried to point out that it was her mother and not herself who had come to seek help. The man ignored her protestations, saying nothing until they came to the wagon. Then he made her get up on it, holding back the cloth screens to let her through.

Beyond, in a tiny enclosure, there was a table with many strange things on it: little glass tubes, white tiles marked in squares on some of which were smears of blood, dishes and jars containing coloured liquids. There were also two chairs, one this side, one that side of the table.

A man in Receiver robes with his hood thrown back appeared from between the hangings that concealed the rear part of the wagon. He instructed her to sit down, taking from a pad on the table a sharp needle which he jabbed without warning into the ball of her thumb.

She gave a little cry, and the Receiver who had escorted her uttered a few words of mechanical reassurance.

There followed a sort of ritual whose meaning she did not understand. The blood from the needle-prick was taken in a glass tube and smeared on the white tiles; then some more was dropped into a jar of coloured liquid; then more still, which had to be squeezed out, was taken out of sight into the back of the wagon. Incomprehensible sounds followed—humming like insects', a gentle clattering, muttered comments in near-whispers.

The man with his hood thrown back returned and gave a nod to the other man waiting at Soraya's side. He had brought with him another needle, which he drove into the fleshy part of her forearm—once more without warning her.

Eyes pleading, Soraya mutely sought an explanation for all this.

"There is nothing we can do for your mother," said the man who had brought her. "We have said often and often that the aged are beyond our help. Sickness must mostly be overcome by the sufferer; we can best help those who have youth and strength on their side."

Soraya's ears were full of the rushing of blood.

"However, by the same token, that makes you very lucky," the Receiver said.

"What?" Though the beginnings of tears she gazed up.

"You are young enough to be helped, and it is still early in the course of—"

"*What?*" She leapt to her feet. "*I'm* not sick! I—I—"

The rushing in her ears gave way to ringing; the cloth walls, the tall black-garbed Receivers, everything seemed to swirl around like water in a stirred pot.

She collapsed.

With great apprehension Firdausi saw the Receiver returning alone from their wagon. He glanced at Soraya's mother and saw she had drifted back into coma. But where was Soraya?

"I have good and bad news for you, young man," the Receiver said, coming close.

"I—don't understand!" Firdausi stammered.

"Your girl-friend has come to us in good time, and we will accept her."

"But—!" His mind froze; his eyes sought a key to this mystery on the Receiver's face.

"I presume you will be entitled to accept the payment we customarily make?" the black-robed man encouraged, and lifted into sight a heavy jingling bag which could only contain the crude soft metal which served as currency here.

Greed fought with amazement in Firdausi's baffled brain. That bag looked heavy—the size of a rich girl's dowry. Nonetheless, he choked out, "But her mother?"

"She is old, and past our help."

There was a moment of silence. Then he said with a surge of determination, "But Soraya is fit and well!"

"You think so? Then come with me!"

Dumb, he complied, and trailed the Receiver across the square to the space before the covered wagon. There, his astonished eyes met the spectacle of Soraya, being carried down the steps to be laid on a pallet on the ground. There was absolutely no mistaking the tremors that racked her slender young body.

The quakes. The dread killer was afflicting her as it had done her mother.

"In our care, there is hope for her," the Receiver was saying. "If you are fond of her, you'll raise no objection."

Firdausi wasn't listening. He barely felt the tug on his hand as the string of the metal-heavy bag was looped around his nerveless fingers.

Nonetheless, since it was the only consolation he was likely to be offered, he finally clutched it to him.

XI

Alarm lights were already flashing and bells sounding discreet but insistent warnings everywhere in the hospital when Nole came running full pelt to join Langenschmidt and Maddalena outside the entry to master operations control.

"I've alerted as many of the staff as I can reach," he panted. "Not many, of course—we don't maintain a night schedule normally. And this isn't the kind of emergency we have drills prepared for. What exactly happened?"

Langenschmidt explained how they came to spot Bracy on their way to join him in the computing office. Nole gave a comprehending nod.

"He must have been looking in at one of the regeneration rooms—probably the end one. There's a woman in there who lost her right hand in an accident at the main repair dock last week. What this fisherboy was doing out of his own room, though—that's what I can't understand. He seemed very tired and perfectly co-operative when I checked him earlier."

"I'll make a guess," Maddalena said sourly. "He didn't want to miss his one and only chance of seeing over the premises."

"That doesn't matter," Langenschmidt cut in. "The fact is he's gone down that tunnel there, and it's taking him where he can cause one hell of a mess if he's not stopped quickly."

"Where does it lead?" Maddalena demanded.

"I told you, didn't I? The hospital's power-plant is down there, all its automatic service controls, all its supplies of things like activated water, oxygen, life-sustaining nutrient flows, artificial tissue-synthesis—the whole lot."

"Why in the galaxy, then, do you just leave the tunnel open like that?" Maddalena exclaimed, astonished.

"Anyone likely to come this way in the normal course of events is a Corpsman, and too sensible to pry into dark corners," Langenschmidt grunted. "I'm going to have your hide, Nole—you realise that, don't you? Leaving the kid in an unlocked room!"

"Yes, but—" Nole recognised the futility of making excuses, and turned away.

Men and women were joining them now from every direction, one or two in the same self-sterilising whites as Nole, the majority in casual clothing, having been routed out of their quarters or called back from recreation.

Langenschmidt briefed them crisply on the situation. Dismayed, they exchanged glances.

"Is there any risk of him doing deliberate damage?" one of the earliest arrivals inquired.

"No, but he's probably in panic. He ran as soon as he saw us. Any suggestions?"

For a moment there was silence. Then an elderly woman who had apparently left the solar therapy room to come here, for she wore only a muslin thigh-length shift, spoke up.

"Not more than two people to go after him, wearing respirators, and carrying cylinders of some anaesthetic would be easier than trying to reason with him."

"Great," Langenschmidt said. "Let's—"

"Just a moment," Nole put in. "How about the radiation?"

"What?" Langenschmidt blinked. "We're on fusion, aren't we? What radiation?"

"I have a couple of cases at the moment in need of isotope treatment. I'm processing iodine-131 and potassium-40. I'm not saying he will, but he might go too close to the bombardment source."

"Marvellous," Langenschmidt said bitterly. "So we don't just go after him looking like monsters—we go looking like mechanical men, in armoured suits. Well, if it's got to be done, it's got to be done. Volunteers?"

"I'll go," Nole muttered. "My fault."

Bracy Dyge was hardly thinking at all now. The effect of irrational terror had been multiplied a score of times in his mind by the combined impact of the drugs he had been given and the violent expenditure of energy while he was fleeing from unnamable horrors. To find himself among machinery—seemingly without end, floor to ceiling—which at any moment might devour him as the naked woman behind the window had appeared to be being consumed, was more than the fragile web of his self-control could stand. He was moaning and panting as he stumbled around the banked machines seeking a place of safety.

When he first came down here, it had been dark, but some distant switch had been turned and now the whole huge room glowed with sourceless light. Was there no shadowy corner for him to skulk in?

Movements at the corner of vision terrified him; lamps signalling on instrument panels made him jump. Even the high-ozone smell, indicative of the immense power slumbering within the apparatus, was fearful to him who had never before been so near a fusion plant.

Gasping for breath, he halted on a gleaming panel set into the floor, which was warm to his bare feet, and heard a noise behind him. Jerking his head around, he saw two white, bulky forms like distorted human beings approaching noiselessly, carrying what his fright-warped eyes interpreted as guns. He screamed wordlessly and ran forward again, randomly, to begin a deadly game of cat-and-mouse all over the big hall.

It was not long before his remnants of cunning discovered that there was one place where his pursuers were reluctant to go; twice, he saw them sidle away from a large black machine the body of which was a metal tube as long as his arm, with thick power cables snaking away from it across the floor. Why they avoided it, he couldn't guess, but as soon as he found a means of doing so, he dived for this tabooed zone.

But those attending him had not bothered to remove the chrome ear-ring he wore, once they were satisfied it was adequately sterile. As soon as he came in range of the eddy-currents surrounding the machinery, the metal heated up. It was as well Cyclops was not so totally backward as still to use metal tooth-fillings, for the effect on those would have been agonising. As it was, he felt as though he had been seized by the ear-lobe in a pair of red-hot pincers, and screamed, and incontinently fled back towards the door.

And that was where they gassed him down, but not before he had acquired a dose of hard radiation sufficient to strip the other half of his head bare of his prized black hair.

"We got him," Nole said unnecessarily as the limp body was placed on a trolley for removal to the wards. "But he'll be one sick boy for at least a week."

"You're an idiot, Nole," Langenschmidt said in a tone-less voice. "That's only the start of the trouble. How about the family he's said to have left in Gratignol? Now we'll have to send them some sort of relief, and if we don't gauge it exactly right we'll have half the poor fisherfolk of the planet begging for handouts to match those given to this one family . . . Hell, that's my worry, and it can wait for tomorrow. I'm getting tired, you know? I've had a pretty wearing time lately, and dealing with emergencies when I ought to be catching up on lost sleep isn't helping me any!"

Nole hesitated. "Uh—don't you want to know about the data I got on Kolb's leg?"

It seemed like last year, instead of an hour earlier, when they had set out to the computing room to inspect these curious findings. Langenschmidt ran a weary hand through his hair.

"Okay, I guess so. But there's not much point, really. I can hardly take any action before the morning, and even then—oh, I'm *rambling!* Hurry up, then, before I keel over and take my nap on the floor!"

Following him down the corridor with Nole, Maddalena found herself regretting that she had ever uttered her contrary opinion when Langenschmidt told her about the ZRP controversy. The pleasure he had felt on seeing her had masked the toll the problem had taken from him. Now, she was coming to realise that if it affected him so deeply she had no right to judge it on the basis of her own miserable experience on a single ZRP—which, after all, she had chosen herself, with her eyes open.

"Here's the print-out," Nole said, with a kind of eager nervousness perhaps intended to disguise his embarrassment at letting the Dyge boy get out of his room and cause so much bother. "You'll see it come in three sections. First off, I asked for a local identification—in other words, for a likely point of origin on Cyclops."

"And got a zero reading, hm?" Langenschmidt's brow was furrowing; he seemed to have recovered a little from his fit of exhaustion.

"That's right. The gene-type is non-Cyclopean, you may take that as definite. His other leg, from which I took a comparison sample, is local and quite common.

"Now the memory does contain a list of those worlds—some eight or ten of them, I believe—where donor-grafting is still accepted medical practice. Some cultures regard it as an honorable thing to permit part of one's body to continue in service after one's death. But there's nowhere within about thirty parsecs where this applies.

"Anyway, I got another zero out of that line of inquiry. So I set for all-galaxy parameters, and I got nonsense!"

He made an impatient gesture at the print-out, and Langenschmidt read it through very slowly and carefully.

"How many's that? Ninety-some worlds?" he grunted.

"Ninety-two—but blazes, look at them, will you? Highest probability, which isn't a match even so, is Earth! And who would conceivably have got Kolb a limb-graft from Earth?"

"What do you think, Maddalena?" Langenschmidt demanded.

"Unless things have changed beyond belief," Maddalena said slowly, "no Earthborn person would consider letting part of his body be exported after death."

"But that's not the whole story!" Nole rapped. "The computer was hesitant about assigning these locations. The correspondence is marginal. And the direction in which the variations are significant is ridiculous! I could print the information if you want, but it's highly technical."

"We'll take your word," Langenschmidt said. "Just make it a bit clearer, will you?"

"Well—uh—one could say that the direction of the anomalies is away from the human."

There was a puzzled silence. Maddalena broke it. "It couldn't be a synthesised prosthetic, could it? I've never heard of such a thing, but it seems a reasonable suggestion."

Impressed, Nole gave a nod. "You mean a limb synthesised to an approximate specification, instead of regenerated to make a match with the opposite limb? It could be, it just could."

"But is there anywhere to your knowledge where such a technique is employed?" Langenschmidt asked.

"No . . . Though with the logjam we have in scientific communication these days, that's not conclusive. If you like, I'll have the data sifted and give you a verdict in the morning."

"You do that," Langenschmidt sighed. "Right now, I want to call it a day. I'm sorry I fouled up your first evening here, Maddalena, because I was really intending to give you a good time."

"What? Oh!" Maddalena had clearly not been listening. "That doesn't matter, Gus. But before we go, can I just check out another idea I had a moment ago?"

"Why not?"

Maddalena looked at Nole. "Can you fix an Earthside location with your equipment? In other words, can you determine the areas where the correspondence is closest?"

"Earth's population is pretty damned mixed," Nole said, staring. "After all, every single gene-type in the galaxy is found there, barring a few late mutations."

"I'm pretty mixed myself," Maddalena agreed impatiently. "Iberian, Amerind, and who knows what? But check, will you?"

Nole shrugged and put the question to the machine.

"Below the limit of acceptable probability," he announced. The closest approach is—uh—how do you pronounce that? Iran, would it be?"

"Gus," Maddalena said, barely audible, "there was a second language on Zarathustra, wasn't there?"

"Of course there was! You've been speaking a bastard cross between Irani and Galactic for the past twenty—"

Langenschmidt broke off, his face going milk-pale.

"Dr Nole," Maddalena pursued, "did you compute your findings with non-civilised gene-types as well as civilised? I'll wager you didn't!" A trifle maliciously, she added, "I'm referring, of course, to the ZRP's."

Nole gave a strangled gasp and revised his instructions to the machine. Almost instantly there was a fresh print-out.

"Probability seventy per cent plus or minus two," he reported. "No, I'm afraid you're wrong, in that case—

which is a relief. The reading would have to exceed eighty to be actionable."

"Even if we turn out to be dealing with ZRP Number Twenty-two?" Maddalena said softly.

There was a frozen pause. Then Langenschmidt clapped his hands and exploded. "Maddalena, how have I managed without you for all this time? Nole, where the hell is the nearest communicator? Maddalena, you're a genius—*damn* you!"

XII

Looking slightly dazed, Nole stared at Maddalena while Langenschmidt waited for his communicator connection to be made.

"Number—Twenty-two," he said, as though weighing the statement for some elusive additional meaning. "I'm sorry, but I'm not yet sure what you mean."

"Oh, come now!" Maddalena snapped. "If you weren't so worried about Gus's threat to have your hide for letting the fisherboy get loose, you'd have seen it before I did. That leg of Kolb isn't regenerated and it isn't original. So it's got to be either a graft or a synthesised prosthetic. You said yourself you didn't know of anywhere the latter technique was being applied, though it's perfectly feasible. So it's almost certainly a graft.

"You said—again—you don't know of any nearby worlds where they make graft material available. Moreover, the computer virtually rules out the chance of a gene-type corresponding to the tissue of the leg occurring on any planet near Cyclops. But it does suggest that the ultimate origin of the ancestral strain might well have lain in the Iran area of Earth.

"At the time when the Zarathustra nova took place, some ten or twelve per cent of the planet's population were of predominantly Irani stock—enough to support their own language as a minority tongue against the pressure of Galactic, and to develop a Zarathustran dialect with Irani admixtures." Maddalena checked. "Stop me, by the way, if I'm ploughing old ground for you."

Nole shook his head quickly. "Candidly, even though at least half the patients who get sent here for major overhaul have been on the ZRP's, I've never really studied the events which led to the present situation."

"You should," Maddalena said grimly. "The ZRP's are the most significant single factor in this sector of the galaxy. But never mind—this'll help me to get my theory straight to my own satisfaction.

"Where was I? Oh yes. Traditions preserved on ZRP One indicate that the incredible number of three thousand ships carrying well over two million people probably managed to lift from Zarathustra—from the night side, which was protected from the fury of the nova by the mass of the planet for several hours after its inception.

"We've located to date twenty-one refugee planets on which people have at least survived, even if only at the most primitive level. But these account between them for a mere ten per cent of the rumoured three thousand ships which got away—in fact, just about three hundred and six. On ZRP One, for instance, we know that precisely two ships landed; on Fourteen, only one. On Thirteen, where I've spent two decades, about sixty made landings—the first arrivals left a subradio beacon in orbit, and others homed on it. Which was a disastrous mistake; the casualties hit eighty per cent in the first year, and despair overwhelmed the remainder to such a degree they still haven't made a full psychological recovery. But I'm digressing.

"The essential point is this. Since the episode on Fourteen with which Gus and I were involved twenty-odd years ago—the time when a gang of Cyclopean entrepreneurs were led by a failed Corps probationer to deposits of radioactive ore there, and used the local people as slave labour to exploit them—we've kept so keen a watch on the known ZRP's that the chance of outsiders from space being able to pull another such trick is negligible.

"On a hitherto undiscovered ZRP, though, all the facts would fit neatly. The gene-type of that graft would correspond well with an isolated group of refugees, from

Irani basal strains, and one of the reasons why the Corps maintains its base here is that Cyclops is conveniently located for the entire volume of space through which the ZRP's are scattered."

Nole's face was haggard and pale. She broke off and gave him a look inviting comment.

"In other words," he said, "you think someone from Cyclops is using an unknown ZRP as a—a spare-parts bank."

"Exactly," Maddalena agreed.

"But that's murder!"

"Of course it is, if they're killing the original owners of the organs they're taking. But don't think murder is so shocking to all human beings as it is to you! Where I've just come from, assassination is a recognised political weapon—and here on Cyclops, Gus tells me, one child in eight doesn't survive its first year. When life is short like that, it becomes cheap."

That was too much for Nole. A Corps medical officer was of necessity dedicated to the preservation of life no matter what the cost to himself. The theory Maddalena had put to him was too cold-blooded for him to endure. He excused himself with a whisper and headed for the nearest convenience to overcome the nausea which had revolted him.

"Where's Nole off to?" Langenschmidt demanded, turning away from his communicator.

"By the look of him, he needs to vomit!" Maddalena shrugged. "I've been explaining to him that Kolb's leg was probably cut off some poor devil on a lost ZRP, and he's upset."

"Not surprised," Langenschmidt grunted. "Though he's by no means a practical man—witness what he allowed to happen tonight!—he's a nice guy at heart, and a damned good doctor. But for pity's sake, Maddalena, don't go spreading this notion of yours broadcast, will you? There are all kinds of possibilities we have to elim-inate before we can act on the suggestion."

"Such as?" Maddalena said sourly.

"Well, the most likely is this one you put forward yourself—that the leg is synthetic. This would be much easier to do than a normal regeneration job, you realise, and probably within the capacity of medical computers such as you might find here. I'm having a search of the data initiated to determine whether Nole's right in say-ing the practice is unknown. If it is, I'll be surprised."

"Why? The number of worlds which can't afford full regeneration techniques is strictly limited, and of those, damned few would support a short-term stopgap ar-rangement—they'd rather go for the advanced method as soon as possible."

"I guess so," Langenschmidt sighed. "Nonetheless, I'm making the check. I'm also requesting the latest informa-tion on all the known ZRP's. I've asked for fullest details on the gene-type records which the Corps has made."

"But you think I'm right," Maddalena pressed him.

He was silent for long seconds. At last he gave a reluc-tant nod.

"I hope you're wrong, blast it! To have another scan-dal on Cyclops will give me headaches for the rest of my tour as Commandant, and if we find out that this is a collective-guilt case, so we have to administer punitive measures, we shall be living here like an occupying army."

"Is that likely?"

"Yes and no. The mass of the people, insofar as they understand the ZRP problem, sympathise with a plight which so nearly resembles their own. Otherwise Quist wouldn't have popular support for her campaign against the policy of non-interference, and she certainly does. So a dirty business like this could scarcely be public knowledge—and indeed if it were we'd have stumbled on it before.

"But Kolb's isn't likely to be an isolated case. And we still have here a top twentieth of the population who've reached positions of wealth and power by ruthlessness. I said this to you earlier, didn't I? And if you find being callous pays, then you're quite likely to feel that some primitive survivor on a ZRP is—is a null quantity. Who the hell cares what becomes of him so long as I'm made whole?"

"The pattern would be similar to that in the Carrig affair, then?" Maddalena hazarded. "A small group would be in full possession of the facts, but because what they have to offer is so valuable, those who benefit from it won't investigate what they're getting—turn a blind eye, as they say."

"What?"

"Turn a blind eye. It's a phrase that's survived on Thirteen, where there are a good many eye afflictions. I believe it's pre-galactic in origin."

"Prehistoric, I'd have said," Langenschmidt muttered. "Except on the ZRP's, I've never seen a blind person. When eyesight is so valuable, it's worth taking the trouble to preserve."

"Hmmm . . ." Maddalena cocked her head. "You said Kolb's isn't apt to be a unique case, didn't you? Would it be possible to find out whether any of the 'top twentieth' of the people of Cyclops have made unexpected recoveries from serious injuries or illnesses lately? Failure of their eyesight strikes me as a good starting-point."

"I *must* be tired," Langenschmidt said. "Or else life on this damned planet has sapped my intelligence. I should have thought of that myself. I'll get the matter looked into in the morning. I don't think there's much I can do tonight. It's gone midnight, you realise?"

"I've been keeping Corps time for the past few weeks on an airless base-planet," Maddalena said tartly. "I've got out of gear with natural day and night." But the reference to the lateness of the hour made her stretch absent-mindedly and repress a yawn.

"What action do you propose taking if my guess turns out to be well-founded? Will you hold Kolb here instead of letting them take him off to this local doctor—Rimerley, I think the name was?"

"Of course not!" Langenschmidt snapped.

"But he's the only evidence we have—"

"He's a two-edged sword," Langenschmidt interrupted. "To use one of the archaic phrases you seem to like! If I do hold him instead of sending him off to Rimerley, it'll be like sounding an alarm bell. You can bet that Rimerley is involved, to start with. He'll signal the team collecting material on the ZRP, they'll pull out instantly, and even if we do locate the planet we'll never find proof of any connection with Cyclops apart from a tenuous link via the gene-type of the tissue. And short of finding the rest of the original owner, or his surviving identical twin, we'll never bring the matter to trial."

"You're quite right, of course," Maddalena confirmed. "Will you wait until they actually bring the new graft down for him?"

"If we can spot that being done. Which I doubt. I expect we'll have to locate the ZRP and catch the collectors red-handed. And I don't have to tell you what a job that'll be!"

"I don't even see how—" Maddalena checked. "Oh yes, I guess it could be done, at that. It must be possible to find out the high-Irani areas of Zarathustra, and compute the most likely courses which ships leaving that part of the planet would have followed. But it'll be the devil's own problem, even then, and the search might take months."

"Years," said Langenschmidt succinctly. "Damn it, we're searching for ZRP's all the time, and if we haven't found this one by now, it must be in a highly improbable corner of space."

"How could the Cyclopeans have found it, do you think?"

"Shall we ask them when we catch them?" Langenschmidt snapped, and was immediately repentant. "Sorry! I didn't mean to bark at you like that."

"No, I'm the one who should apologise. After all, it's still only a suspicion, and I've no business pestering you as if it was already proven. And you are tired. I'll leave you in peace. Will you have me roused in the morning in time to see Kolb collected? I'd be—interested."

"Surely," Langenschmidt agreed, and gave her a weary smile which she returned with warmth.

As she was walking away, he called after her.

"Maddalena!"

"Yes?"

"Too soon to ask your views on non-interference again, huh?"

"*Now* who's treating my suspicions as a proven fact?"

"Right." Langenschmidt smiled again, with greater naturalness this time. "Good night. And—it's good to see you after all this time."

"In spite of all the trouble I've brought with me? I'm flattered."

XIII

"Get away from that girl!" rasped Lors Heimdall.

The two members of his team who had been bending over the unconscious form of Soraya jerked and spun around. They had drawn back the light coverlet to expose her high, youthful bosom and flat firm belly, and the next stage in their plan took very little deduction to work out.

"What's wrong with you?" the older of them grunted. "Are we getting a high price for virgins this trip, or something? It's not going to make any odds in the long run!"

"Get the hell out of here!" Heimdall thundered, and tugged aside his black robe to reveal the butt of his energy gun.

The two men exchanged glances, shrugged, and complied.

Heimdall re-belted his robe and wiped a trace of sweat from his face. He dared not tell his subordinates just how necessary it was to get the girl home in perfect condition; one hint of the danger they had all been running since Kolb was taken to the Corps hospital, and they would desert forthwith.

Still, luck was on his side so far. To have got his hands on the girl, the very same day he received the request from Rimerley, was remarkable, and had greatly built up his confidence. Of course, she was rather dark-complexioned, like nine out of ten of the inhabitants, but there were ways of eliminating the melanin secretion which caused that. And in every other respect she was close to perfect: the right build, the right proportions, the right category as regards immunological reactions. . . Rimerley had said, in view of the importance attaching to this job, that he was prepared to accept far less adequate material and work it over to the required specifications; so much trouble would not after all be necessary.

He bent to spread the coverlet over Soraya again, and paused with his hands grasping the cloth. Of course, it was quite true that in the long run it wouldn't matter—no actual physical damage would result, apart from the inevitable minimum, and on any world with reasonable sexual standards that would have been sustained within a year or two of puberty, while as to psychological damage, that was absolutely irrelevant.

He blocked off the train of thought with determination, however, and threw the coverlet back to its former position. Then he crossed the room and seated himself before the carved wooden chest which concealed the subspace communicator.

Rimerley had been waiting tensely for the call ever since Kolb was brought in and he finished making his checks of the man's condition. As he had expected, he was in amazingly good shape considering what he had been through less than one full day earlier—the Corps hospital offered treatment which Rimerley simply had no facilities for.

But the facilities he could offer had brought him immense wealth and not inconsiderable hidden power. Now was the time to use that power, to protect himself.

The moment the call came, he knew from the expression of near-gloating on Heimdall's face that the worst of the risks had passed: that resulting from delay in making the key proposition to Quist.

"You got someone?" he rapped, leaning forward excitedly.

"I think so," Heimdall nodded. "I haven't yet found the material for Kolb, but—"

"The hell with that," Rimerley interrupted. "We can attend to Kolb at our leisure. First we have to make sure the leisure happens!" He peered at the corner of the screen, where a draped body was dimly visible, slightly out of focus, beyond Heimdall's shoulder. "Is that the girl behind you?"

"That's the one. We had to bring her in by giving her a phoney attack of the local killing disease—the quakes, as they call it—but she's over the symptoms now and in artificial coma. In view of the circumstances, we weren't able to find out much about her barring what her boy-friend told us, but it is definite that she's no older than her midteens, and all the items which you listed for me when you put in the request appear to be satisfactory. She even has the right blood-group, which I gather you were worried about."

"Has she? That's amazing!" Rimerley felt tension go out of him like air from a punctured spacesuit. "The commonest groups on Cyclops seem to be the least common out there. I take it you're sending her home straight away?"

"I was wondering, in view of the urgency, whether we ought not to risk bringing the ship down directly to some point near here. The chance of it being seen—"

"Isn't worth taking," Rimerley cut in. "No, even if it means a day's delay, transport her by inconspicuous means to the usual landing-area in the hills. There remains a slight chance of being caught, you know, and the compounding what we've done by exposing a ZRP to open contact with space-travel is a needless additional danger."

"I've always assumed they'll throw the book at us if they catch us," Heimdall grunted.

"I've had this out with you a dozen times," Rimerley countered. "There are enough worlds offering voluntary euthanasia for us to make a case— Just a moment! Have you told the girl anything?"

"Haven't spoken to her since we gave her the fake disease, of course!"

"Hm . . . We'll have to convince her, for the sake of appearances, that she's deathly ill and better off enjoying a quiet demise."

"We've done that successfully more times than I can count," Heimdall commented with a cynical smile.

"Yes, but—Hell, why I'm wasting time *I* don't know! I'm going to see Quist now. Wish me luck."

The message was brought to Quist during the second session of the day's conference. Dr Aleazar Rimerley was waiting to see her at her earliest convenience.

Damn the man! Picking this moment to come—and in person, for some inconceivable reason! A communicator would have served for any message, surely!

She bit her lip, looking around the conference hall while the servant who had brought the message waited discreetly at the back of her tall chair. The morning had seen the last of the differences of opinion between delegates ironed out to acceptable levels; this afternoon, there had been several much-applauded suggestions for lines of action to secure a reversal of the non-interference policy. Two of them even, in Quist's view, offered a better-than-fifty-fifty chance of succeeding: a record.

Omar Haust hadn't shown up after his disgraceful exhibition of last evening. Maybe that had something to do with it—delegates from wealthy advanced worlds always seemed to be uncomfortable in the presence of a genuine ZRP native.

The speaker who had the floor at the moment sensed that something was amiss. He paused courteously and looked at Quist. So did everyone else.

Cursing again silently, but keeping her face composed, she stood up.

"I'll beg your indulgence," she said. "A very dear friend—as some of you may have heard—was savaged by a wolfshark yesterday."

A murmur of sympathy spread around the meeting;

she saw one or two baffled expressions, but seat-neighbours of those who didn't know about wolfsharks soon explained.

"I'm told that the doctor attending him wishes to see me urgently. If you can forgive me—?"

"Of course!" exclaimed a dozen voices, and she slipped away with a bow.

Rimerley was waiting for her in an audience room with delicate silver-filigree walls. The setting seemed particularly appropriate to the most highly reputed medical man on the planet, Quist thought, and her irritation at being summoned away from the conference gave way to anxiety at Kolb's condition. If Rimerley had come here in person, that might all too easily mean bad news.

She said, "Doctor, is it something about—?"

He cut her short brusquely. "Before we discuss anything, I want your assurance that we are neither overheard nor recorded."

"Doctor! I assure you—"

"Save it. I know that no one gets to the heights you've scaled on a planet like ours without being very cautious and far-sighted. But caution says we talk privately about the matter I've come to raise with you."

She stared at him. Previously, Rimerley had treated her with urbane courtesy—even obsequiousness. Now he was addressing her not merely as an equal, but even as an inferior. The last statement was an order: gift-wrapped, but an order nonetheless.

Colouring, she snapped, "I prefer not to be spoken to in those terms!"

"I know. But if you care about Justin Kolb, you'll have to put up with it."

There was a pause. Finally she shrugged and crossed the room to the far side. Lifting one of the elaborate filigree decorative motifs, she exposed a small switch and twisted it through ninety degrees.

"All right. The record will show nothing now, not even the fact that I came in to join you. What is it you want to say? Have you—have you attended to Justin yet?"

"No. Oh, there's nothing to worry about as far as he's concerned—the Corps doctors did a good first-aid job on the stump and it'll heal quickly."

The reference to a stump made her flinch. To cover his out-of-character weakness, she countered him harshly.

"How soon will he be well? And why, if that's all that's been done to him so far, have you left him directly after taking him into your care?"

"There's nothing I can do until we find a graft for him," Rimerley said. And waited for his meaning to sink in.

"A graft?" Quist listened to her own repetition of the word, as if it were mere noise. "But I thought you used regeneration. Isn't that what it's called?"

"For a woman who's been the effective government of a planet for so long, you're astonishingly ignorant," Rimerley said. "I'll cheerfully regenerate the limb for you—if you'll buy me a megabrain-capacity medical computer to do it, and pay for having it stocked with the appropriate data for Cyclops. Since you can't afford to do that, Kolb will have to get the same as he did before: a limb-graft, which is easier and cheaper."

"Before? You mean—"

"I'm coming to what I mean. And it's going to take a lot of explaining, so I'd better sit down." Rimerley glanced around for a chair and did as he said.

"Graft!" he continued. "The taking of an existing organ and the incorporation of it into another body. Clear? You gave me Justin Kolb with a leg lost to space-gangrene, and I replaced it with a nearly perfect match, immunologically neutral, the nerves and muscles tied in as well as might be hoped. Not well enough for him to endure the strain of space-side work any longer, but this wasn't a drawback you'd object to in view of your—uh—relationship."

"Rimerley," Quist said between clenched teeth, "I don't know what you're getting at, but—"

"Then wait till you find out!" Rimerley ordered. "Yesterday that leg was being attended to by Corps doctors. I have no way of knowing whether they looked at it closely enough to determine its origin, but if they did, you're in trouble. Apparently you didn't actually know that limb-regeneration was beyond our facilities; it's common knowledge, however, and it would be assumed that you connived at what was done—"

Quist was waving a feeble hand, floundering two sentences behind Rimerley's urgent flow of words. "Origin?" she forced out.

"Yes, *origin*. What do you think I did—bought the leg off some dockside layabout in Gratignol, maybe? Even a starving fisherman wouldn't be likely to sell a healthy limb, would he? No, it was imported. From somewhere where none of the natives can spread the news—to be precise, from an unnumbered ZRP."

Quist's mouth worked, but no sound emerged.

"I was going to say," Rimerley pursued, "no intelligent outsider would credit that you, Alura Quist, imagined I'd regenerated the leg! You must have known. And what happens to your precious conference, to start with, when the word gets out?"

The prospect of this news reaching the delegates was appalling. Quist clenched her hands into bony fists.

"This is blackmail!" she whispered. "You won't get away with it! I'll denounce you—I don't care what happens to Justin. Maybe the Corps will mend his leg when I tell them about—"

"Denounce me? It'll look like panic to save your campaign against the Corps, and they won't fall for it! Besides, the Corps will have other things on their minds. After what you do to them!"

She gave him a blank stare.

"The Corps might—yes, just possibly *might* heal Justin Kolb as a generous gesture," Rimerley conceded with a judicious air. "But they won't offer you a new lease of life, as I will. You're afraid of old age, aren't you? You're afraid of death, and the long dark silence beyond."

There was something so evocative of terror in the words that Quist found herself nodding numbly.

"So now we come to the point," Rimerley said. "The proposal I have for you, which is to the advantage of both of us. I don't want this story to get out, even though you'd be the worst sufferer. I'm saving my own skin, and I won't deny the fact. But the chance of the Corps being sufficiently intrigued by Kolb's leg to make investigations depends on what else they have to occupy them, and you're in a position to give them a problem which will drive everything else into the background— for good, let's hope. What's more, I see from the news reports on your current conference that you've already prepared the ground for what I want you to do."

He added, offhand, "Kolb will get his leg back too, of course."

Quist was absolutely frozen for long moments. Finally, in a voice drained of emotion, she said, "What, then?"

"What I offer?" Rimerley countered. "Oh, nothing much. Twenty years of additional youth. Maybe fifty!"

Greed blazed in Quist's eyes for a moment, until it was extinguished by tears. "It's a cruel joke!" she said hoarsely. "It's the foulest, dirtiest—"

"I'm *not* joking." Rimerley leaned back in his chair with such complete calm she was again tempted to believe him.

"How?"

"That I'm not telling you. Yet. I'm simply making the offer. Twenty years, possibly a lot more." He studied her with insolent directness. "How's the unsupported shape of your breasts these days? Flabby, I imagine! And the belly-muscles must be giving way by now, in spite of cosmetic treatment. I could fix all that."

Once more, silence filled the room. It dragged on and dragged on. Rimerley broke it, shrugging and rising.

"Too bad. I didn't really expect you to prefer public humiliation and probably trial for an infringement of the laws against interference with ZRP's. Which will be a very ironical climax to your campaign, won't it?"

"Wait," she whispered. "Damn you! You knew there was one bribe I couldn't resist!"

"Of course I did," Rimerley said with a sneer.

"What—what do I have to do?"

He told her, in a single crackling sentence, and added, "Today!"

XIV

As promised, they had fetched Justin Kolb away early in the morning. Maddalena saw him go, in a white-painted hospital 'copter which went droning towards the southwest. Its design struck her as somehow archaic, but after twenty years in surroundings absolutely devoid of technology beyond crude tool-making, she found she was ill-attuned to refinements in engineering practice.

"I wish there was some way we could have put a tracer on him," Langenschmidt had muttered as he stood beside her, gazing at the diminishing white speck against the vivid blue sky.

"I'd have thought there was!"

"I asked Nole what a reasonably thorough medical check might overlook, and he said, point-blank, 'Nothing.' Rimerley can't be incompetent—his patients have included some of the most notable people on Cyclops."

"Did you ask Nole how it was in that case he came to overlook the nature of Kolb's mended leg?"

"As a matter of fact"—Langenschmidt looked slightly uncomfortable—"I did. We had some words about it. But the point stands; no tracer, for fear of alerting them."

"Surely you know where he's going, though."

"Allegedly, to Rimerely's private island. But I'd be happier if I was convinced of that. As you said last night, he's our evidence."

"You've kept some tissue-samples, presumably."

"Nole took some from places where they wouldn't be noticed, and they're preserved as a calibration standard for this analysis of gene-types he's doing. At least, that's our story if the matter comes up." The 'copter had vanished. Briskening: "Well, I can't stand here all day. I have a base to run."

"I haven't," Maddalena said demurely. "And since you had me brought to Cyclops, I guess there's something you can have me do instead of 'standing here all day'."

"Actually there are a couple of things . . . I wasn't very eager to ask you, since it seems unfair when you're theoretically on long furlough, but as the subject has come up—"

"You're a poor diplomat, Gus, in spite of your boasting. Well?"

"What spare time I have right now is generally taken up with studying the progress of this damned conference of Quist's. The local news bulletins are full of it, painting it as an unselfish venture by Cyclops on behalf of their poor brothers neglected by the rich greedy worlds of—etcetera; why should I tell you what you can imagine easily enough? There was some kind of outburst at an official banquet last night—the delegate from ZRP One got drunk and uttered a few home truths which embarrassed the organisers dreadfully. Catch the reports of the morning session of the conference, will you? Let me have a digest of their progress if any at the noon break. That's one thing. And the other is of your own making. Go help my overworked programming staff to get a line on the probable location of Twenty-two. We probably won't get the margin of error lower than a hundred parsecs, but if we can possibly shave it to fifty I think I can swing the assignment of a couple of search ships."

The problem was fascinating, and intensely complicated. It was known what the populations distribution had been on Zarathustra at the time of the nova, so it was possible to determine which of the high-Irani areas would have been on the day side and hence wiped out immediately. On the night side, however, there were three notable zones where the minority language was spoken, and in any of these such a gene-type as they had found in Kolb's leg might have occurred.

With this as a basis, it was then necessary to compute whether one or two or all three stood a chance of getting people from their homes to the nearest spaceport before the planet turned far enough on its axis to expose the rising ships to the nova. Only those which had been able to keep in shadow of the planet for several million miles had escaped the storm of radiation.

One of the key zones had been in darkness for a full seven hours; the other two, for a mere half of that.

Settling on that as the most likely course of events, the team instructing the computers then had to work out what trajectory ships would have followed to remain in shadow if they had stayed till the last moment picking up refugees; if they had left with an hour to spare, or two hours, and so on, backward through the Zarathustran night. And from these hypothetical lines of flight, they attempted to calculate where they would have wound up.

The process went smoothly for a while; several possible courses were at once ruled out because the Corps had explored the volume of space through which they led, to the extreme range any ship could have covered with its passengers in a fit state to endure a landing. After that, though, it was like plodding through heavy fog and deep mud.

Maddalena complied with Langenschmidt's request to hear the local news bulletins about the conference; they were platitudinous, merely giving extracts from pious speeches interlarded with praise for Quist's and Cyclops's noble compassion towards the ZRP's. Listening, she was reminded of what Langenschmidt had said last night, when he asked if it was too soon to re-question her on her attitude towards the non-interference policy.

She was no longer sure what her attitude was. And to

find this reaction in herself so soon after her arrival here was disturbing.

She was glad to lose herself again in the complexities of interstellar course-plotting, and was deep in what appeared to be a promising assumption when an urgent message came through to the computing room for her: would she go see the commandant at once?

Reluctantly she complied, framing a jocular complaint to utter when she saw Langenschmidt. It died on her lips. One glance told her he had been badly shocked by something.

"Gus!" she exclaimed. "You look as though you've just heard this sun is going nova too!"

"Next best thing," grated Langenschmidt. "At any rate, it's having the same effect—we're compelled to evacuate."

"*What?*"

"Sit down and I'll play you back a recording of the news. I couldn't trust myself to repeat it coherently." He slammed switches on the desk at which he sat, and a screen lit. Maddalena moved numbly to a seat from which she could see it properly.

At first there was only a blur, with an automatic voice-over signal identifying the time of reception and dating it on the basic Corps scale; then the blurring faded, and a harsh incisive voice with a Cyclops accent rang out.

"Personal and official from Alura Quist to the Commandant, Corps Galactica Repair, Refit and Recreation Base, Cyclops. Alura Quist!"

A face appeared on the screen. Maddalena studied it with interest; this was the first time she had seen the famous Quist, who had for so many years been undisputed arbiter of this planet's fate. She saw a pretty blonde woman whose best attempts to stand off the effects of age had not entirely succeeded.

"Commandant, you will learn from the appended

recording of my address to the Conference on Non-interference with Zarathustra Refugee Planets at which I am currently presiding what it is that you are required to do. I only wish to add that action is to be taken forthwith to implement the decision of the government of my planet."

The face vanished, and re-appeared, this time in the context of a large conference hall, in which sat delegates from worlds affecting over a dozen different styles of dress. Quist was addressing them, and had clearly won the approval of all those listening.

"You will recall," she was saying, "that the respected representative from ZRP One—who is regrettably indisposed and cannot hear me make this public pronouncement—suggested a lever to oust the Corps from its role of policy-maker in this area. I have reflected on what was suggested, and come to an inescapable conclusion: it is not consistent with our professed ideals to tolerate the Corps's presence here while they are flouting our wishes."

Stunned silence, from the audience in the screen and from Maddalena.

"I therefore wish to inform you that I am serving notice today on the base's commandant to withdraw all Corps personnel from Cyclops and close the base. This cannot presumably be done overnight, but it must be done quickly, and in any case from this moment forward the base will be quarantined, and all contact whatever between Cyclops and the Corps Galactica will cease barring such official conversations as the evacuation may call for. I—"

Stormy applause drowned out the remainder of the statement. Langenschmidt snapped the switch to stop the replay.

"Well?" he rapped.

Maddalena shook her head, dazed. "I thought you said the planet couldn't afford to lose the base!"

"It can't. Which means the Quist woman has gone insane. Insane or not, though, she's legally the boss of Cyclops, and when I get word from Corps HQ—which I've sent for—I'm damned sure they'll tell me I've got to do as she orders."

XV

Langenschmidt's gloomy assessment of the situation was justified; his own computers assured him of that even before a verdict came through from headquarters. No inhabited world was compelled to provide facilities for the Corps. To obtain those which it needed and could not adequately arrange on the airless lumps of rock where most of its bases were sited, the Corps wrote treaties like an independent sovereign planet. But it wasn't one, and in the event of a planetary government deciding that it wished to withdraw leased territory, the decision was unilateral and unarguable.

When the legal experts from HQ informed him of this situation, Langenschmidt railed at them, demanding why such a predicament had not been foreseen and guarded against. There was a chilly tone in the voice of the man he was talking to as he retorted that the circumstances were unique and unprecedented, and after all he—the base commandant on the spot—had been in the ideal position to do the foreseeing.

Sweating, Langenschmidt cut the connection.

But that crack was still ringing in his memory the next morning when he went out on the main pontoon of the repair docks to meet the official Cyclopean representative he had been warned to expect. This was a very tall, very thin, very bitter young man in immaculate white uniform, who stepped down the gangway from the big skimmer which had brought him and even before Langenschmidt had a chance to speak waved a brisk hand at the men who had gathered on the vessel's deck as she approached the pontoon.

"My staff," he said. "Empowered by the government of Cyclops to supervise the evacuation of Corps personnel."

Langenschmidt looked them over. In all, they numbered at least two hundred. Like a good many worlds whose economy was too precarious to support full employment and too poor to pass the leisure barrier beyond which working became irrelevant for the individual, Cyclops made the worst of both worlds by maintaining a government labour force analogous to the pregalactic armed forces of Earthside nation-states. These would be a detachment of picked men drawn from that pool.

They were armed, Langenschmidt saw sickly, with obsolete but doubtless workable energy guns. Quist *must* have lost her mind!

"And matériel?" he snapped.

The tall thin young man blinked at him. "My instructions are not definite on that point," he replied. "I am simply to see that this base is evacuated of all its personnel within a reasonable time. Unofficially, I'm to inform you that the government regards seven days as reasonable."

"*Seven days!*" Langenschmidt hadn't meant to let the exclamation go, but he could not restrain his dismay as he surveyed the immense repair docks and all the buildings beyond—a complete self-contained city, with some of its foundations including those under the space-drive test-beds going clear to the bedrock of the planet.

"Seven days," the tall thin young man said, and gave a cadaverous smile. "My name is Bengt Barly, incidentally. I hold the rank of major in the Cyclops space-force."

"Hold tight," Langenschmidt told him savagely. "You're apt to drop it any moment."

He swung on his heel and signalled one of his subordinates.

"This is *Major* Barly," he snapped. "No doubt he would prefer to deal with someone of his own status. Certainly I'd rather he did so."

Barly coloured bright pink, which gave Langenschmidt a moment of gloomy satisfaction. But that was the last such moment he enjoyed for some time.

What possibilities were open to him, other than complying with the edict of the government? His superiors said there were none; ships would be detached from other posts and sent to conduct the evacuation in the speediest and most efficient manner available resources would allow. And that was that.

He drove fist into palm in helpless fury. Clearly, the only recourse was to overset the Quist government—and how could he do that? If only they had delayed this lunatic expulsion order another couple of days, long enough to pile up concrete evidence on the matter of Kolb's leg!

Which reminded him that Maddalena hadn't shown up this morning. He looked around vaguely for her, but she wasn't to be seen, and immediately his other worries drove her out of his thoughts.

Overset the Quist government . . . This was the obvious lever. But already, during the night, radar-carrying vessels had encircled the base island, and a ship had gone into stationary orbit at twenty-three thousand miles, watching through sensitive detectors for any breach of the rule that there was to be no contact whatever between the Corps and the rest of Cyclops. Even a submersible wouldn't get away to hunt the evidence Maddalena had suggested and check on rich Cyclopeans who had made miraculous recoveries lately. After all, even the Bracy kid's trawler had an electronic fish-finder, and submarine detectors would certainly be watching the nearby waters—

The trawler!

He stopped himself, by a tremendous effort, from turning to look at the ramshackle craft, with its peeling paint and torn solar sails which were in fact currently being replaced by a robot to which no one had remembered to give contrary orders.

Hmmm . . . ! But the idea was only a germ so far, and there still remained his other obligations: more inescapable ones. He shelved the problem of what could be done with a sure method of escape from the island, and went to attend to another pressing matter. It derived from one of his unsuccessful pleas to headquarters; begging for orders to decline Quist's ultimatum, he had suggested that this was a plot to get the Cyclopeans' hands on the material resources at the base, and perhaps set up a commercial starship repair service with what they inherited.

The staff of Corps HQ were sufficiently cynical for that to register. But they didn't change their instructions. They merely recommended the installation of a new switch, radio-controlled, on the main fusion generator buried at the island's heart, so that as soon as the personnel had been evacuated what was left could be reduced to a smoking crater.

That would be a small consolation. Sighing, Langenschmidt set off to rout out his chief power engineer.

Maddalena had thought of the trawler much sooner—last night, to be precise, while restlessly trying to doze off. She had also taken into consideration the fact that, not being on the established strength of the Corps here, she figured in the computer records only as "personnel on leave" and a tap on a computer keyboard could abolish her without explaining where she had gone.

These points led her to pester Nole for half an hour, until in sheer desperation he allowed her what she wanted: to see Bracy Dyge, in private.

When she opened the door of his room, the fisherboy cowered back like a frightened animal, doubtless having taken the shaving of his head—part of the treatment necessitated by his exposure to an overdose of radiation—as a prelude to some terrible punishment for his temerity last night.

It took all Maddalena's experience as a diplomat among primitive peoples to bring him to the point where he would listen to her without trembling. Time was wasting; she had to seize her hard-won advantage.

"Bracy," she coaxed, "didn't you say when you first came here that you had always dreamed of working for the Corps?"

The boy's answer was inaudible; she had to wheedle for minutes to get him to speak his mind honestly. Then what he had to say was hardly promising. She damned Nole for the sarcastic reception he must have given the boy's reluctant plea; it had closed him up tighter than a Pelagian clam.

She was forced to make wild promises and offer wilder bribes—not to him: for his family, which was more honourable—before she got the assurance of his help. Langenschmidt wouldn't like this, but then he might well not like any of it.

The door of the room slid aside, and there he was.

"Beat me to it again, did you?" he muttered.

Maddalena was bewildered for a moment, and then she started to laugh. "You mean you thought of it too?"

"Of course I did!" Langenschmidt rapped. "Did you expect me to lie down under the edict of this damned idiot Quist? Nole told me you were down here, and I immediately saw why I'd had that boat of Dyge's on my mind all day, in spite of the swarm of Cyclopean officials crawling over the base like bedbugs."

"Well, it's no good to you, is it?" Maddalena countered. "Your chance of staying behind on Cyclops is zero."

"I could swing it so that—"

"Could you, *hell!* The protocol of the evacuation of a Corps base traces all the way back to the abandonment of a sea-going ship on Earth. I'm closer to my Corps training than you are, by a long way. You've probably forgotten the irrelevancies you pick up in training—like that one—but there's the regulation if you care to check: the commandant is the last to leave the base, and the person responsible for handing over control to the successor authority."

Langenschmidt gave a groan. "They planned this to drive me out of my mind with frustration! But what good is the boat to you?"

"If you'll let me finish what I was saying to young Bracy here, you'll see soon enough." And, turning to the fisherboy, who had listened with blank incomprehension to this exchange, she resumed, "Now if you had good maps, and perhaps a radio, you wouldn't mind sailing half around the planet, would you?"

"I'd sail to the stars if I had a ship," Bracy declared with a sudden fit of braggadocio.

"I believe you. You're a brave boy—*man*. Anyone could tell that after hearing how you killed the giant wolfshark. Now here's your chance to prove it still further, and to do the kind of job which will interest the Corps in you, as well as earning you that new set of solar sails, and a new set of reactors, *and* a radio for your ship." Maddalena eyed Langenschmidt as she spoke, and received a shrug to indicate that if the Corps was leaving behind much of its matériel here at the base it could afford to give Bracy a few such odds and ends.

The coaxing went on, the flattery, the cajolement. Langenschmidt's mind, greatly preoccupied, went darting away. If only they had waited till this business of Maddalena's "undiscovered ZRP" had been cleared up . . . Was it coincidence or not? Oh, surely it must be! True, Rimerley was in the space parts trade up to his neck—must be, as the surgeon who performed the graft on Kolb—but surely he couldn't have a hold over Quist sufficient to compel her to act this way! The existence of a link between them wasn't proof of criminal complicity. Even if he was blackmailing her because she knew the source of Kolb's new leg, that alone wouldn't make her jeopardise the planetary budget of Cyclops for the indefinite future. As soon as the drawbacks of losing the Corps' rent began to be felt, she would be done for anyway. Someone else would overthrow her government and more than likely invite the Corps back. In which case, perhaps he shouldn't blow up the base—repossessing a workable installation was one thing, rebuilding a pile of rubble was another, and progress over the past century had probably made the job uneconomic.

Running the base here wasn't as challenging as maintaining his old Patrol beat, but it had its own rewards, and he had enjoyed the work.

If I do leave here for good, he told himself sourly, *I can go two ways—back to headquarters to serve as the walking spokesman for a computer, or out of the Corps. Or else I can jump in space.*

He grew suddenly aware that Maddalena was addressing him, and muttered an apology for his rudeness.

"I was asking," she repeated with a twinkle, "whether you've booby-trapped the island."

"How did you—? Oh, I guess it's an obvious precaution. Yes, I have, but with a radio-activated trigger."

"Don't be in too much of a hurry to press the button, then. Bracy here has just agreed to smuggle me out of the area and around the world to Rimerley's private island, and with his help I may very well give you back your job when the Quist government falls in the wake of the row I'm cooking up."

"You?" Langenschmidt said.

"Yes, me!" She gave him a defiant stare. "Gus, the reason I've been hanging around making up my mind what to do with my furlough is perfectly simple. I don't want to 'rest up' on Earth or any other soft-centred planet. I've been doing damn-all for twenty mortal years. I want some action to get my blood flowing again—and here it comes!"

XVI

"What's that—object over there?" inquired the insufferable Major Barly, gesturing.

Langenschmidt turned, hoping that his personal concern with the "object" would not show. The sun lay bright and full over the gleaming hulls of the vessels from space currently in the repair dock, making the contrast between them and the tiny, dirty trawler all the more marked. Around the fishing-boat, robots and men were busy in a manner that could not be glossed over except by a half-truth.

"That?" he said with maximum smoothness. "Oh, you'll recall that Justin Kolb—Quist's friend—was rescued from an encounter with a wolfshark. That trawler belongs to the boy who saved him. We don't want to exacerbate relations with the populace more than we can help, so we thought we'd overhaul it for him while he's recovering from his experience."

Major Barly's opinion was clear from his expression: Only idiots would concern themselves with one worthless fisherboy at a juncture like this. However, he vouchsafed his gracious permission to carry on, so long as it did not interfere with the speedy departure of all Corps personnel.

It was lucky, Langenschmidt reflected, that Quist had sent them a fool to supervise the evacuation. Maybe there were none but fools in the Cyclopean government forces, but that was doubtful. An intelligent man, Langenschmidt suspected, would have wondered what was amiss when the base commandant—so gruff and ill-mannered on first meeting—suddenly turned extremely affable and insisted on spending the entire working day escorting his visitors over the base, snapping at subordinates who seemed reluctant to comply with the Cyclopeans' requests, apologising for any delay longer than two minutes, and in general being co-operative to the point of parody.

Registers of personnel were printed out of the computers; roll-calls were taken to ensure that no one slipped away unaccounted for; ships were called in from nearby stations to orbit Cyclops until the moment—scheduled for day six after the ultimatum—when loading of personnel and salvageable goods would begin.

Damned if I don't think I made a mistake in running such an efficient base, Langenschmidt told himself glumly. *If I hadn't given strict orders to the contrary, I think we could have done the whole job in two days flat.*

Meantime, while he cast around for new ways of stalling the Cyclopeans, two significant tasks were in progress. A friendly executive of the Corps personnel branch, back at headquarters, was tracing one Pavel Brzeska, on promotion furlough following his tour as commandant of the Patrol sector which included Langenschmidt's old beat—normally, Langenschmidt preferred not to have more truck with generals than he could avoid, but this was a special case—and some highly interesting work was going on at the dock, under the rough wooden deck of Bracy's trawler.

Already it had had enough trickery and gadgets crammed into its small hull to make it the envy of the richest fishing family in Gratignol. If there was room for all the machinery Maddalena had specified as "potentially handy", it would wind up being the envy of the richest private yachtsman this side of Earth.

Not that the said yachtsman would ever get to hear of it.

By the evening of Day Two, as Langenschmidt was now mentally labelling it, both these matters arrived at a

satisfactory conclusion. The trawler would have to make
its departure as openly as possible, so there was no question of a night sailing—a waste of several hours, but on
the other hand no matter how fast the ship could potentially travel it would have to dawdle until it was beyond
the watchful ring of Cyclopean forces, which would
make the start of the trip very slow anyway. Maddalena
was closeted with Bracy, training him in some of the
techniques the rebuilt vessel would call on him to em-
ploy.

And the call came through from Pavel Brzeska. Langenschmidt, having made quite certain that the Cyclopean inspectors would be kept away for an hour or
two, took it in his villa.

"Gus!" the new general exclaimed as the connection
came through. "I just got the news of the pickle you're
in out on Cyclops! What possessed you to get backed
into a corner by that crowd? You've tangled with them
before, haven't you? During the affair on Fourteen, I
seem to remember."

"That's right." Langenschmidt nodded. "With Maddalena Santos—who's here, by the way; I sent for her because of the Conference on Non-Interference with
ZRP's they're holding."

"Heard about it. The first time Cyclops has made the
news in the Old System since its original breakaway
from Dagon, I imagine. There's a powerful lobby working on the subject, and a good deal of sentimental propaganda being splashed around." Brzeska scowled. "What
does it look like from the Cyclops end, anyway?"

"Much the same as those we've had before—pious and
empty. But listen, Pavel! What I need you for is something more or less related to the ZRP's, and with your
background you can tell me a lot of things I daren't obtain conspicuously through normal channels. I'm going
on a string of suspicions, and though I'm morally certain

I'm right I can't call for full Corps support without more solid evidence."

"Explain!" Brzeska commanded.

Langenschmidt did so. He wound up, "It's been very tricky trying to complete the calculations involved, of course—we have to keep taking the Cyclopean inspectors in and out of the computing rooms to check on manifests and personnel registers and so forth. But by—uh—a bit of dodging we've managed to narrow the search area in which the missing ZRP must lie down to a fifty-parsec sphere. Who do I ask to loan me some ships to find it?"

Brzeska scowled again, this time ferociously. "Damnation! What's become of the Corps in your sector since I came home? Time was, if a suspicion like yours blew up, they'd assign you the entire Fourth Fleet and no questions asked!"

"If they hadn't issued this ultimatum to me, I'd have been in a position to make the request officially. As it stands, the assumption is that I'm costing the Corps its base here through incompetence, poor intelligence and general mishandling of relations with the local government."

Brzeska eyed him keenly. "I know. There's a three-member commission of inquiry on its way to you—should reach you just about in time to see you leave, if this one week's grace stands. And—ah—*did* you foul things up that way?"

"I did not. I took it for granted that Cyclops wouldn't cut its collective throat. Without the income from the base their planetary budget will go to hell in two years."

"I know."

"I didn't realise you'd made a special study of the matter," Langenschmidt said with some bitterness.

"But I have," Brzeska countered softly. "It was touch and go whether another commandant was appointed after your immediate predecessor, or whether the base should be closed as obsolete and superfluous. The dependence of Cyclops on the revenue from it tipped the balance. Actually, when they consulted me I advised continuance—I went there on local leave and enjoyed some wolfshark-hunting when I was younger."

"It sounds as though I picked the right man to contact," Langenschmidt said, pleased.

"You certainly did. Now—let's see . . ." Brzeska stared at nothing for a moment. "Oh yes. You want Keita Bakary, at my old base. He'll fix what you want in short order."

"Thanks very much. What I do plan to do, incidentally, is slip away under the pretext of being called to a top-level conference on the redeployment of personnel from here and the selection of a substitute base-location, and by the time they finish investigating the circumstances I should have the rope braided to hang Quist by the neck."

Brzeska shuddered visibly. "You pick some unpleasant similes, Gus. Must be the effect of your long-time contact with the ZRP's. Well, I wish you success, and a speedy return to your base."

It was still quite dark, lacking another hour till dawn, when Maddalena stole down the steps to the dock at which Bracy's trawler was moored. A tightly co-ordinated plan to distract the attention of the Cyclopean inspectors, nodding at their guard-posts, ensured that she reached her goal safely and was able to slip below unnoticed.

There, she laid herself down in a concealed compartment just forward of the engines and ran a quick check of the new instrumentation which had been fitted. All seemed to be in perfect order. She repressed a chuckle due to sheer exhilaration and spoke in a whisper to the microphone she wore taped against her vocal chords.

"Gus! I got aboard—no trouble—and your engineers have done a magnificent job on the boat. I don't know where it's all been put, but one still has so much room I was afraid at first sight something had been left out!"

"If you really want to know," Langenschmidt answered in a tinny buzz from the bone-conduction receiver Nole had fitted to her, "they took out the original lining of the hull and replaced it with solid-state and printed circuitry. Be careful not to foul any rocks—a dent in the hull could put a dozen gadgets out of operation."

"If you wanted to hit a rock with this kind of nav equipment, you'd have to aim deliberately—and at that the automatics would probably overrule you." Maddalena made reflexively to brush back her hair, and remembered belatedly that last evening she had had it trimmed to the regulation Patrol length of one inch—as a safety precaution when wearing a space-helmet. She wasn't sure why, but a set of space-kit was among the gear she had asked to have put aboard.

"Just a second," from Langenschmidt, and then: "That was Nole. Bracy is now awake and they're checking him over. His condition last night appeared good, but you'll have to make sure he continues to take drugs against the dose of radiation he received. Also he doesn't like the flavour of our standard high-vitamin rations. I tried him on synthesiser cake and he likes that okay, so he'll be coming aboard with a portable diet-synthesiser—a 'farewell gift' from his friends in the Corps."

"Barly will probably take it off him," Maddalena said sourly.

"He won't get the chance. I obtained his permit to clear the trawler for open sea last night, and then Nole fixed him—uh—a liquid lullaby. He'll sleep till noon."

"A shame. I had as much as I could stand of synthesiser cake away back when on Fourteen. Well, all I have to do now, I guess, is wait."

"Exactly—until you're hull-down away from the last of the Cyclopean ships watching this area. And then—swift journey!"

Maddalena gave a throaty laugh and signed off.

Bracy Dyge played his part magnificently, Langenschmidt had to admit. He came down the steps to the dock with just the right mixture of regret at leaving the comfortable island and the luxuries the Corps enjoyed, and eagerness to try out the new solar sails and mended fish-finder which were the official extent of the modifications to his boat.

"There was no call to go to such trouble for the kid," said one of the Cyclopean inspectors, a man with a face like a lemon whom Langenschmidt had preferred not to fix a name on in case it was as ugly as he was. "I'm sure Alura Quist will see he gets properly rewarded."

"I'm sure," Langenschmidt agreed blandly, forbearing to mention that if all went well Quist would be getting a reward of her own quite shortly.

He was almost holding his breath as the trawler eased out to open water, with Bracy proudly waving at his new solar sails. Then he relaxed. In two hours, or three at the most, the boat would have passed the outermost circle of quarantine vessels, and then some remarkable changes would come over it.

The solar sails would be furled, and a pair of hydrofoils would extrude from a hidden compartment under the hull, and the compact fusion reactor which had replaced the old stored-power accumulators would feed power to the pipes—and the trawler, shaking a little, but perfectly sound after what the engineers had done to it, would take off for Rimerley's private island at a comfortable hundred and fifty knots.

Quite neat. *Quite* neat. He only hoped he would have

been able to wipe the grin from his face by the time he next had to confront Barly and explain about the need for his departure to attend this important conference about a base to substitute for the one being closed down.

XVII

That voyage was among the most extraordinary experiences of Maddalena's chequered life. She had hung from the talons of a parradile; she had dropped through atmosphere with nothing but a spacesuit's reaction jets to save her from a fatal crash; she had canoed over rapids and ridden all manner of odd beasts of burden. But streaking across the oceans of Cyclops was perhaps the weirdest journey of all.

To start with, the news that a Gratignol trawler—last seem limping along at a typical speed of a few knots—was outrunning all but the fastest passenger skimmers plying between the more densely inhabited islands would certainly have alerted someone's interest if it had been noised around. Accordingly, whenever the automatic detectors spotted another vessel in the vicinity, they cut the power and spread the solar sails. Bracy and Maddalena then sat out idly on the deck looking as though they hadn't a worry in the universe bar the shortage of oilfish in these waters. The danger past, the power returned, the sails furled, and once more they leapt towards their goal at the front tip of a mile-long jet of heated water.

Bracy, although he had been very willing to start on this mission, and at the outset was delighted with what had been done to his craft, grew bored within a few hours. Maddalena had shown him the operation of everything, including the devices which had no connection with seafaring, in order to entertain him, but the fact that control of his vessel had been given over to machinery disturbed him, and he sat with a worried expression staring at the wake and listening with head cocked to the hum of power emanating from below.

What was chiefly worrying him, Maddalena puzzled out at last, was not being able to see where they were going with his own eyes; he had known of radar, of course—some of the wealthier fishing-families in Gratignol could afford both it and a fish-finder, whereas the poor families had to settle for the latter only—but the little screen was no psychological equivalent for eyesight.

It was, naturally, out of the question to go on deck with a hundred-fifty-knot wind howling past them; they were only able to sit in the after cockpit because the fairing over the cabin had been subtly altered to make it aerodynamically efficient at these speeds. But when Bracy showed signs of real distress at this headlong career, she decided they might risk running for a while on manual control, to show that the ultimate responsibility had not been ceded to the machines.

That was almost the last decision she took in life. Some enormous marine creature—not a wolfshark, but nearly as large and quite as solid—showed up on the fish-finder, and seeing such a huge obstacle dead ahead Bracy yelled with alarm and put the helm hard over. The boat dipped its side in the water, because the foils could not cope with such a violent change of direction, and for half a mile they skidded in a tight circle with spray streaming over the deck and great shuddering slams of water battering the hull.

By the time Maddelena got the helm away from him and let the boat straighten of her own accord, the cause of the trouble was miles astern. But that was the last attempt the fisher-boy made to control his craft at its new maximum velocity.

Especially when they were compelled to slow to avoid comment on sighting other ships, Maddalena had a good deal of time to talk to the boy, and by the end of the voyage had come to like him a great deal. Faced with such problems as he had, many youths would have given up at once; instead, orphaned, with nothing but this trawler as a means of livelihood, he had grimly set out to replace two healthy, hard-working adults with decades of seafaring experience. That sort of thing took guts of a different kind than those needed to save one from panic at the sight of strange armoured figures chasing a hospital patient through a nightmare of menacing machinery. She had thought of him entirely as an instrument, a way to escape the surveillance of the Cyclopeans and follow Kobl to Rimerley's island; now at last she came to see him as a person—shy, ambitious even though trapped by circumstances, and intensely proud.

Also, handicapped as he was by his overdose of radiation, he had the kind of tough persistence legend attributed to the pre-galactic coolie who, half-starved, half-frozen, dressed in rags, had maintained unstoppable energy.

By the time they came over the horizon to Rimerley's island, and accordingly had to slow to typical trawler speed to escape notice, she had extensively revised her original plan and spent a couple of hours before nightfall and the landing in briefing him with the new instructions.

It was ironical that they should be able to drift with the current here, in plain view, Maddalena thought as she surveyed the doctor's private domain. So much the better, though—to have had to wait till dark before coming into line-of-sight would have imposed extra difficulties.

With a powerful magnifying periscope which had been built into the mast of the trawler and projected a needle-sharp image on a screen at the bottom, she studied the prospect before her. Clearly, Rimerley was one of Cyclops's "top twentieth", as Gus Langenschmidt called them—indeed, he must be among the thousand wealthiest men on the planet to maintain premises like these. A huge house, part of it extending out into the ocean so that one could enjoy the sensation of being in a vast aquarium by descending a short flight of steps; a private dockyard with two skimmers at the quay; a 'copter parked behind the house, and beyond that a road winding up to the topmost point on the island, where trees concealed the ground.

If it was true that he had built his fortune by selling the spare parts of human beings, he must have run through scores—possibly hundreds—of victims, Maddalena thought, and the realisation made her stomach churn with nausea.

Faint from below came the sound of martial music, and then a voice too muted for her to catch the words, but having a distinctly coaxing tone. Bracy was playing with the radio again. Though his family had had one before his parents died, he had had to sell it, he told her, during the hungry month of last winter, and in any case the one which the Corps had fitted aboard the trawler was far superior to any in Gratignol.

She continued her study of the land ahead, looking for signs of life. Some turned up: a man came back from taking in fish-lines, carrying a large basket of gleaming sea-creatures; a man in white, probably a mechanic, came out to attend to some job on the 'copter and went into the house again.

"Bracy!" she called.

"Just a moment." There was a pause, and then he put his head out of the cockpit. "Yes?"

"I'm sorry—were you listening to something?"

The boy's lip curled. "A government announcement. The man was saying how the closing of your base would make life more difficult, but we must think of our poor brothers on the refugee planets. What I want to know is, why are they so eager to have more poor people to cope with when they can't even give us a decent living?"

Good question, Maddalena commented silently. During the voyage Bracy had plied her with questions about

Cyclops and other planets, and had shown a surprising degree of natural insight into the problems they discussed. Most likely, Maddalena assumed, his parents had been comparatively literate as Cyclopean fisherfolk went, and had done their best to pass on their education to their son.

"You wanted something?" Bracy added.

"Yes. I want to find out if there's any communication going on between the island and some other part of the planet. There's a device for doing that among the equipment below. I showed you how it works—do you think you can remember the details?"

"Yes, I think so. If I can't, I'll be honest." He gave her a flashing grin and vanished again.

She chuckled, resuming her examination of the island's image. Shortly, he called back to her.

"No, there are no communicators operating as close as that. The nearest is over to the eastward—I think it's a pleasure-boat acknowledging an alteration of schedule."

"Good—thank you. Now how about internal communicators?"

"Right!"

And within minutes: "Maddalena! There's a conversation going on I think you might like to hear."

She rose in a lithe movement and dropped through the open hatch. A voice was coming from the remote tapper which enabled eavesdropping on room-to-room communicators at distances up to ten miles.

"—everything ready by midnight," the crisp words rang out. "Now there must be no delays! I know I always say that, but tonight is more crucial than usual, even. We must have the entire job finished within half an hour."

A different voice said, "With this quarantine and embargo business, what happens if they recognise an unscheduled landing and take it for a Corps intrusion?"

Maddalena tensed.

"They won't!" the first voice snapped. "It's not an un-scheduled landing. This one is for Quist, remember? And I got her to have it officially scheduled. I don't know what it's being called: luxury goods for private consumption, I think—"

An appreciative though fawning laugh broke in, and a muttered, "Very good, very good!"

"So!" the first speaker said. "Anything else?"

"No, I guess not."

"Get on with it, then."

The tapper went silent; there were no communicators in use on the island any longer.

"What was all that about?" Bracy demanded, staring.

"Something is going to be brought down from space, for Quist," Maddalena said. "At about midnight. That much is clear, but exactly what—"

She broke off, a light dawning. Langenschmidt had mentioned to her his half-formed suspicion that the ulti-matum for evacuation of the Corps base might be con-nected with Kolb's leg and the risk of its origin being discovered, but he had been unable to see what link could compel Quist into action. Suppose, though, it wasn't a matter of compulsion, but of bribery; suppose she was due to become one of Rimerley's customers for the renewal of some failing organ—from her recorded image at the Non-Interference Conference it was plain she was no longer youthful—and Rimerley had told her that she would lose her chance if the Corps cut off the supply of spare parts . . .

"That *must* be it!" she exclaimed, and ignoring Bracy's bewilderment she dived for the subspace communicator which was her link with the Corps. The bands it used were untappable, as far as was known, by any equipment on Cyclops, but just in case Corps intelligence was faulty in that area there was an automatic scrambler on the cir-cuit as well.

"Maddalena Santos," she said as soon as she had her

connection. "I want to speak to Commandant Langen-schmidt."

"I'm sorry," came the smooth reply. "The commandant has been called off the planet for a conference on redeployment of base personnel."

"Damn—already? Then give me whoever's acting for him."

"Dr Nole is the senior officer at present on duty, but he's engaged with the Cyclopean inspection team at the hospital. Is there anyone else you wish to speak to?"

"Not particularly," Maddelena sighed. "Wait a second, though, I have an idea. Can you record a scrambled message and get it to Langenschmidt for me?"

"Yes, certainly. Just one moment." A series of clicks; then—"Go ahead now, please. Recording."

In terse words Maddalena summed up her suspicions and ended, "By the way, Gus! Since you're so sure you'll be back as soon as the Cyclopeans feel the pinch, why not try and con the authorities into assigning this evacuation fleet to search for the unknown ZRP, instead of just tamely spreading our personnel here over a dozen bases and leaving it at that? It's going to take at least thirty ships to shift what's being lifted away—half that number could carry out a thorough sweep of the high-probability locations.

"Of course, knowing you, that's probably exactly what you're doing at the moment."

She closed the message and thanked the Corps operator. Then she turned to Bracy.

"Can you use an energy gun?" she demanded.

The boy shook his head.

"I think I'll pass the next half hour teaching you. Whatever's being brought down here at midnight is valuable, and if we interfere there may be trouble. Lucky I brought a spare gun along, isn't it?"

XVIII

Darkness closed around the boat, still drifting as any fishing-boat might when awaiting the arrival of a shoal along the line of a nutrient-rich current.

"That makes us effectively invisible to the naked eye," Maddalena muttered. "Now let's make ourselves invisible to his burglar alarms, and we can go ashore."

Bracy had tried and failed to comprehend the concepts behind this cryptic statement. He put out his arm passively, and Maddalena strapped a miniature radio beacon around it.

She had programmed a geepee computer for the task of making them electronically invisible, and it was perhaps the neatest trick of all those they were using. Essentially she had shifted frequencies on the tapper and connected both it and the computer to an ultra-tight-beam transmitter. The beacons would show their location at any given moment; the tapper would indicate on what band the detectors were operating, and the transmitter would put out an eddy current, so to speak, which would confuse the circuits in the detectors and cause them to record something as diffuse and harmless as a patch of sea-mist. The fact that slight mist usually followed sundown at these latitudes in summer was an additional advantage.

"Remember, though," Maddalena admonished Bracy sternly, "even if it is pitch dark, and you're masked for the detectors, you can still make noise, and that'll give us away. Be careful."

Bracy nodded and grinned. The grin vanished as he glanced down at the butt of his energy gun, protruding from its water-proof holster. Maddalena felt a twinge of worry—was it wise to have given him the weapon when any instruction had necessarily to be theoretical? She had restrained him from firing it only with difficulty, but she dared not let him see a bolt actually fired—energy guns were not the sort of weapons common fisherfolk could afford, and their discharge was extremely conspicuous, especially over water where they raised a wall of steam fifty or more feet high.

Too late to change her mind now—time was wasting, and well before midnight they had to explore the house, the nearby estate and the high ground behind, among the trees. For that, in Maddalena's judgement, was the only place a spaceship could put down near here, unless it landed on water, and that too was an attention-getting event attended by clouds of spray and high waves.

Almost certainly among the trees, she had concluded. And going at a snail's pace, it would take a couple of hours to carry out their preliminary survey, let alone prepare counter-action against Rimerley and his staff.

"Anchor!" she told Bracy.

Silent as a ghost, he lowered it to the bottom and gave a cautious tug to ensure it had gripped. On his whispered confirmation, Maddalena let herself over the side and, using a stroke that created minimum disturbance in the water, set off for the shore.

There were lights on in the extension of the house that ran along the sea-bed, but the room within was empty. On a low table lay the remains of a meal—the eater, apparently, had had little appetite tonight. Through windows higher up, women could be seen moving about —three of them in all, one in white, the others in dark green gowns.

Maddalena led Bracy some distance along the shore before heading inland. She had already got a clear idea of the layout of the house: the seaward side was the owner's, the landward included servants' quarters and all the domestic and mechanical offices. There seemed to be no trace of children; presumably either Rimerley was unmarried or he maintained a separate establishment else-where. Or, of course, he might be old enough to have children already grown—she had somehow been thinking of him as a young man, greedy and ruthless, rather than an old man, merely callous.

Their first stop was the dock where the skimmers were moored. No one noticed them as they bent over first one, then the other, of the graceful craft. From there, they went to the 'copter. The mechanic was just finishing his job, wiping his hands and putting away some tools. They waited for five minutes to let him get clear, and then Maddalena tossed a small sticky object at the side of the machine. It clung as it touched.

Now, anyone attempting to leave the island by skim-mer or 'copter would attract the unwelcome attention of a homing rocket with a shaped-charge head, unless he was sufficiently observant to remove the sticky objects Maddalena had planted.

Which she doubted. The said person was likely to be in a wild panic.

"Door shut," Maddalena whispered very softly. "Now the ventilators."

The house's air-conditioning system was quite conspic-uous from the trawler: two high circulating stacks led down to the pump-chamber on the roof. Bracy had as-sured her that he, accustomed to grappling with solar sails in unexpected gales of wind, could get to the top easily; nonetheless, she waited with heart in mouth and hand on gun while he scaled the intake stack and placed at the top the three glass canisters tied into a bundle with an explosive cord which she had given him. There was a radio-activated fuse on the end of the cord.

She had been puzzling for some time over the matter of where Justin Kolb would be located; it wasn't until she was planning this job on the air-conditioning that she saw the most likely possibility. Any sensible doctor tak-ing patients into his private dwelling would put them at

the terminal end of the air-circulation system, in case
they had infections which draughts could carry to the
other occupants. As soon as Bracy had come down
safely, she told him to keep watch for her and approached the window of the room adjacent to the base
of the discharge stack.

And there he was, in a large room full of medical
equipment, watching a musical recording and sipping a
cup of wine. No one else was in the room with him, but
there were open communicators on both sides of the
bed, and a medical scanner was focused on his torso.

Her original plan had ended with the location of Justin Kolb and his removal to a point from which the
Corps could send down a ship to retrieve him, and she
was glad that she had acquired information leading to a
change of plan. It would have been far too easy, as she
had envisaged it. Just fire the radio-fuse, wait ten
minutes until everyone in the house was unconscious,
smash a way in to bring Kolb to the boat, and—end.

Tame. This way was much better.

She had seen enough of the house now, and led Bracy
away from it towards the high ground. They kept a
course parallel to the road, but out of sight of it, a precaution she was glad of when a fast ground-skimmer
hummed up from the house to the concealing trees
ahead, and within minutes came back.

The trees were thickly leaved and prickly, some local
species she hadn't been warned about; before Bracy was
able to show her how to avoid the dropping branches,
she sustained several scratches on her face. They made
the last stretch of their journey interminably slow, but at
length they emerged into sight of a small plateau crowning the island.

Maddalena pursed her lips. Even without more help
than starlight, she could see that this was one of the
best-equipped private landing-grounds she had ever
heard of. A squat building dominated it, with an im-

pressive array of antennae on top, including one unmistakable one meant for subspace communication over interstellar distances—a real shock, to find that sort of equipment here. Maybe the Cyclopean government *was* conniving at Rimerley's actions!

And what could it be that was expected at or soon after midnight? A new leg for Justin Kolb? Such a gruesome piece of evidence as that would be enough to convict Rimerley and his associates even in a Cyclopean court, let alone a galactic one!

"What now?" Bracy whispered, touching her arm to attract her attention.

"I'm going to try and plan an ambush for the people who are coming from space," Maddalena told him, equally softly. "I don't know how many there may be of them, nor how many of the staff from the house will come with Rimerley to greet the ship. Those who stay behind, of course, won't pose any problems . . . Oh, damnation!"

She clapped her hand to her forehead.

"What's wrong?" Bracy demanded. He had put on a wolfish grin at the thought of what was to hold back those in the house from interfering—it was a trick that tickled him immensely, especially since he had had personal experience of the same brand of anaesthetic gas when he was cornered in the operations control room of the Corps base. The grin had vanished immediately Maddalena let out her stifled exclamation.

"Rimerley may not come up here by ground-skimmer. He may prefer to use the 'copter, and if he does, it'll be brought down instantly. I'll have to go back and unbug the damned thing!"

"Let me go," Bracy suggested.

She hesitated. But so far he had shown himself reliable, and after all there was little time now . . .

"Okay!" she decided. "All you have to do is get close

enough to take off the sticky thing—you saw where I threw it?"

"Yes. I can do it quickly and come back soon!"

"Good luck!" she shot after him as he disappeared.

Then, furious with her own excess of ingenuity, she set off on a tour of the miniature spaceport, looking for the best hiding-places and points of vantage. To ambush the crew of an interstellar ship with only two persons was a tall order, but there was equipment in the trawler which should make it possible, if she could get back there, collect it, and get it installed in time . . . What was keeping Bracy? Was it necessary to wait for him—could she not meet him on the way back to the shore and save time?

Better not.

The stars crept around the sky towards the midnight configuration, and still no Bracy. With a start she realised that if he took any longer it would already be too late to fetch what she needed from the trawler.

And it was too late! From the direction of the house came the distinctive drone of the 'copter's engines; she could see lights moving around its parking-place, and shadowy figures crossing bright lamps.

It began to rise, and for long moments she was imagining the whish and crash of the rocket which was keyed to home on the sticky beacon. But nothing happened. The 'copter merely turned towards the tiny spaceport.

There was a rustle in the undergrowth beside her, and she spun, hand slapping the butt of her gun.

"Bracy!" the boy said in alarm, and she recognized him. Furious, she railed at him.

"What kept you? Now we have no time to go to the trawler and get what we need!"

"I'm sorry. I dared not go close. They were working on the machine—fitting something like a tray under its belly. In the end I could not wait any more. I caught one of the men, about my size, as he went out of sight of the others, and did *so*." Graphically, he closed his hand on his own throat and groaned. "Then I took his clothes and went openly to the machine to remove the sticky thing. I was just in time—a man of great importance came from the house to see that all was well with the work. So I went back and killed the man I had taken clothes from, and got rid of his body. They looked for as long as I was near enough to hear, but I think they will not find him. There is a wolfshark in the bay—did you see it, earlier?"

"No!" Maddalena exclaimed.

"Yes. Not feeding, not followed by buzzards, but they are always hungry for human meat."

Maddalena digested that information as well as she could.

"What now?" Bracy pressed her.

She shrugged. "We play by ear, I guess."

"What?"

"Never mind. Watch, and listen, and take your orders from my signals. We shall simply have to do as well as we can with two energy guns and the advantage of surprise."

She motioned him silent, for the 'copter was humming down over the treetops, and the last scene of the night's drama was all set.

XIX

As the ship slanted through the fringes of the air, Lors Heimdall wondered grimly just how much of his explanation his men had believed. He'd told them that this deal was so profitable they could afford to return home ahead of schedule, and there weren't likely to be many complaints about that—the natives could get along without Receivers of the Sick for a while, until the next time some death-fearing client put in for a new heart or some wealthy idiot crossed up another wolfshark, like Justin Kolb.

Nonetheless, it was quite unprecedented in the history of their venture to pull the entire team off the ZRP and go home *en masse*.

He'd taken the decision to do this in cold blood. If by any chance Rimerley had been wrong in his estimate of the effect on the Corps of Quist's ultimatum, and some too-nosy doctor had thought to check the gene-type of Kolb's leg, he didn't want to be trapped by the Patrol on a noisome, dirty, mud-grubbing planet not worth a snap of the fingers.

There wasn't any question of cancelling their long-term plans completely, of course. In a few years more, he himself would inevitably become a customer for Rimerley's skilled attentions—sometimes, after great effort, he found it hard to breathe, and knew that his lungs and bronchi were aging. And why should he squander most of his hard-earned fortune on a trip to some prosperous world, for medical treatment, when he was indispensable to Rimerley and could persuade the doctor to overhaul him without charge?

All this aside, though, he did wonder very seriously

138

whether his men had not guessed the truth behind his order to pull out.

It was lucky the trip was such a short one; the ship was crowded, and in a confined space tempers could easily be rubbed raw.

Also there was the girl, who was indisputably attractive. Most of the men hadn't been able to overcome their revulsion against dirt and take themselves a native woman during their stay on the ZRP. Now Soraya had been washed and disinfected, though . . . Yes: the shortness of the journey was something to be thankful for.

"They're waiting for us at the landing ground," the pilot reported unnecessarily. "I'm going straight in."

"You're watching out for Patrol ships? With the evacuation of the Corps base, I'd expected local space to be crawling with them."

"They're over the shoulder of the planet," the pilot grunted. "Two, two and a half thousand miles from where we're setting down."

Not a hitch. Heimdall found himself relaxing from unnoticed tension.

Everything, indeed, went with such smoothness that he was almost disappointed to have wasted so much energy on needless apprehension. The ship settled with hardly a bump—the pilot had become accustomed to rough landings on the ZRP, and this was the next best thing to a public spaceport. Heimdall was already at the port when the all-clear lamps winked on, and the panels slid back to reveal the night outside, and a few glinting lights silhouetting a parked 'copter with a group of four men close by.

"Wait a moment!" Heimdall snapped to those of his own team who were excessively eager to jump down, and called in a low voice across the field. "Doctor?"

"Here I am," Rimerley answered. "You weren't bothered, were you?"

"No, no challenges—nothing. Can you take the girl down in the 'copter? I've kept her in coma all the way."

"Yes, there's a cradle slung for her stretcher. Get her over here quickly and we'll take her to the house. Then I'll come back for you."

"Right!" Heimdall turned and gestured curtly for the girl be carried to the lock. He thought it as well not to tell Rimerley yet that there would have to be at least three trips with the 'copter to bring down all the men who had returned with him.

Soraya was carried by two complaining bearers over to the 'copter and placed in the cradle. Heimdall walked with her, and as soon as the job was done nodded to Rimerley.

"Off you go—but don't be too long over sending back the 'copter, will you?"

Rimerley, edgy, caught a false note in the words, and gave him a long hard stare. Then he walked a few paces away, beyond the pool of light in which the 'copter rested, so that he could see the dim glow of the ship's lock. There were more craning, peering heads in view than there ought to have been.

"Heimdall, have you brought your whole damned team with you?" he rasped.

Heimdall took a deep breath. "Yes. And we're not going back till the pressure is off."

Startled, the men who had come up with Rimerley closed on their boss; similarly, catching Heimdall's words and finding their half-formed suspicions confirmed, everyone from the ship came scrambling out of the lock and hurried to ask frantic questions. There was a babbling argument within seconds, and accusations and counter-accusations poured out as though a dam had burst.

Couldn't be better, Maddalena thought. *That's everyone from the ship outside now. I'll bet on it—there sim-*

ply wouldn't be room for any more. And they said something about bringing a girl with them. From the ZRP, beyond doubt.

She nudged Bracy, who slipped away into the darkness a score of paces, and as soon as he was at his appointed position she rose to her feet.

Her voice rang out with shocking authority, amplified to ten times natural volume. "Stand still, all of you! I am an executive officer of the Corps Galactica, and you are under arrest for violations of the Unified Galactic Code!"

The effect of the roaring order was all Maddalena had hoped for. Long seconds passed with everyone on the port immobilised by shock; during the passage of those seconds, she pressed the little button on a device clipped to her belt and transmitted the signal which would explode the cord tying the three glass cylinders together at the top of the intake stack supplying the house's air. Enough anaesthetic to knock out an army flowed sluggishly down to the ventilators.

Then the man whom she had managed to identify as Rimerley—quicker-witted than his companions—broke from the group and ran hell-bent for the 'copter. Shouts greeted this act, and someone with good sense yelled, "Stop him!"

"Patrol Probationer Bracy!" Maddalena shouted into her loud-hailer. "Disable that helicopter!"

And for pity's sake, do it without injuring the girl slung underneath!

She thought he would never respond, and was lifting her own gun when at last he did.

Perfect.

He had displayed the unexpected good sense not to hurry over this first use of his weapon; he had remained calm enough to sight as he had been told, to steady his arm, hold his breath, and only then let go the bolt.

It blazed across the field, illuminating the entire island

as brilliantly as lightning, and sheared away the rotor from the 'copter just as Rimerley got the power on and turned the blades into a shimmering disc.

Droplets of molten metal shattered the transparent roof of the pilot compartment into shards of opaque plastic, and Rimerley screamed like a frightened beast. But it was unlikely the girl, protected by the craft's hull, had suffered any hurt.

"Thank you, Bracy," Maddalena said at full volume. "The rest of you, stay where you are, and if one of these disgusting butchers makes a move, or tries to run for it, burn him, understood? Bracy, come over and help me disarm them."

There was a powerful psychological impact in the unleashed violence of an energy gun, even to people raised on Cyclops, where violence was far commoner than on most civilised worlds. Sullen, sick-faced with terror, the cluster of men waited as patiently as cattle in a slaughterhouse for Bracy and Maddalena to come up to them. Bracy was grinning all over his face, he was so pleased with his contribution to the night's work; Maddalena had to scowl ferociously before he smoothed his features into a pattern more suited to a probationer on official business.

The technique Maddalena had devised for this stage of the proceedings worked beautifully. Bracy came up to each man in turn, gun in his right hand, palming in his left an anaesthetic capsule with a self-injector attached. He clapped the victim on the shoulder and left the capsule sticking to the flesh while he withdrew any weapon the man had at his belt: in all, four of them had arms. A look of vague surprise would cross the man's face, and he would slump about half a minute later.

Meantime, Maddalena had gone over to the 'copter, playing a handlight on the wreckage. Rimerley was sitting still and moaning. Below him, the girl lay uncaring, long black hair draped over the end of the stretcher.

Hmmm! Very pretty! I wonder if they were going to—to dismantle her for spares!

But she had no time for such gruesome reflections. There was a flash from behind her, and she whirled. The tall, cruel-nosed man who had supervised the bringing of the girl from the ship—Heimdall, Rimerley had called him—had broken from the group and was dashing towards the dark shelter of the trees. Bracy had loosed a bolt at him, and fired wide.

Maddalena's gun was up on the instant, and her bolt did not miss.

Those of the group who were still conscious gaped, and then, in comical unison, doubled up to vomit on the ground. At this range, an energy gun turned a man into a handful of calcined bones, and a smell, sickeningly delicious, of well-roasted meat . . .

Maddalena waited till she was sure Bracy had the situation under control again, holstered her gun, and turned back to Rimerley. He had regained some of his self-possession, and was bleating into the communicator, trying to raise his staff back at the house.

"That won't do you any good," Maddalena said curtly. "I gassed the house and they'll sleep till morning. Come on—get down from there!"

Like a badly operated marionette, Rimerley complied, falling awkwardly and twisting his ankle. He limped when Maddalena ordered him to move towards his colleagues, and made a whimpering complaint about such treatment.

"If you complain once more," Maddalena told him stonily, "I'll take a leg off you, the way you did to the poor bastard who provided a graft for Justin Kolb. Is that clear?"

Rimerley gulped enormously, and began to waddle hastily forward.

"That's the lot," Bracy said proudly, indicating the

scattered forms on the ground. "And I've piled their guns over there."

"Excellent," Maddalena said. "I never thought we'd do it, to be frank. You've been quite amazing." She clapped him on the shoulder, forgetful for the moment of what he had just been doing, and was first startled, then amazed, when he put up his hand anxiously to make certain it was not the end of his usefulness and his turn to be knocked unconscious.

Rimerley, breathing raggedly, fought to recover his dignity. He said, "I demand to know by what right you—"

"I told you," Maddalena snapped. "If you want specific charges, the main one will probably be murder, and the subsidiary, interference with a Zarathustra Refugee Planet."

Rimerley gave an oily smile. He said, "My government contests the legality of the non-interference rule, as you ought to know. And plenty of planets recognise the right of euthanasia. If you're assuming that we committed murder to obtain the grafts we have employed, you're wrong. I can show you a release for each of the donors, agreeing to euthanasia because of incurable illness or serious injury."

"Including the girl over there?" Maddalena countered, and saw with satisfaction the look of horror that wiped away the doctor's smile.

"What now?" Bracy pressed her.

"Well, since they've been so kind as to provide the means," Maddalena said, "I think we might as well go directly to see Commandant Langenschmidt. I haven't flown a spaceship for several years, but I was taught how in Corps indoctrination, and they say what the Corps teaches you can never be forgotten. Want to try space for a change, Bracy?"

The boy hesitated. Then self-respect overcame his

doubts, and he put his shoulders back and nodded vigorously.

"Then help me drag this load of carrion aboard, and we'll leave," Maddalena said.

XX

The ship bringing the three-member board of inquiry from Earth, which had put the parsecs behind it at a speed to make light look like a tired snail, dropped into its assigned slot at the Cyclops base. The three board members emerged: Senior General Lyla Baden, small of build but large of voice, and two colonels—a staff rank, indicating that they had not served in the Patrol, but had spent their entire careers in administration.

"General Baden?" said Dr Anstey Nole, stepping forward to greet them. "My name is Nole, second senior officer here at present."

General Baden looked at her surroundings with an icy blue eye. She said at length, "You're under ultimatum to leave this base by tomorrow at latest, aren't you? Where are your preparations for departure?"

Indeed, it was obvious to the most casual glance that the work of the base was proceeding normally—far from tearing down the installations, men and robots were at work on repair and renovation, a fact which had given the Cyclopean inspectors a bad time recently. It made them feel peculiarly helpless, for there was nothing whatever a backward world like Cyclops could do against the Corps if it decided to dig in its heels.

Major Barly strode forward from where he had been standing, next to Nole. "I want to register the strongest possible protest against the defiant behaviour of your base commandant!" he thundered. "Until yesterday he was according us full cooperation. Then suddenly he turned about and countermanded all his orders, and refused to see me and explain his high-handed obstinacy."

"Hmmm!" General Baden looked him over. "Who are you?"

"My apologies." Barly recollected himself and clicked his heels. "Bengt Barly, Major, Cyclops Space Force, assigned to supervise the evacuation of this base."

"I see. Where is this commandant now? Why didn't he come down to meet us on our arrival?" A chill pervaded the general's words.

"Commandant Langenschmidt is awaiting you in his villa, General," Nole said calmly. "I am asked to take you there at once."

"Carry on, then," the general said grimly. "I shall want an explanation—and it will have to be a good one."

Langenschmidt greeted the newcomers with a mask of inscrutability. He was not alone in the room where he received them. In addition to six armed Corpsmen, there were an aging man who looked to be ill from some cause subtler than disease—possibly fear; a youth who held himself as erect as a Corpsman but clearly wasn't, for his hair was completely shaven, not trimmed to the Patrol's standard inch; a very young girl with dark hair and wide, doe-like eyes full of alarm; and a woman in undress Corps uniform around whose mouth played the suspicion of a smile.

Without preamble, General Baden said, "I'm told by the head of the Cyclopean inspection team that you've countermanded the orders to evacuate. Why?"

Not twitching an eyelid, Langenschmidt retorted, "Because the base is not going to be closed. Furthermore, I intend to ask that the ships assigned to transport our personnel away, which are released from that duty now, be reassigned to me for a special task." He paused. "In fact, I think about half the total number of ships will suffice—the rest can return to regular duty."

"Have you taken leave of your senses, man?" rapped the general, emphasising the last word as though she had long ago ceased to expect intelligence in members of the opposite sex.

"General, if you'd sit down—? Chairs!" Langenschmidt barked, and the Corpsmen moved hastily to bring some. "I think you need only listen to me for a few minutes to see I know what I'm talking about. I'd like to start by introducing all those present, if I may. Ah . . . Maddalena Santos here is attached to my staff for special duties, and I'll be asking you to take back with you a commendation in her name for diligence above the call of duty. But that's by the way. This young man here is a Cyclopean fisherboy from a place called Gratignol, Bracy Dyge; he has applied for probationer status in the Corps and has so conducted himself as to earn my maximum approval for the application."

Bracy grinned broadly and went back to the pastime mainly engaging his attention at the moment: looking at the slender, attractive girl next to him.

"This," Langenschmidt continued, "is Dr Aleazar Rimerley, who is not here under quite such favourable auspices. He is in fact under arrest for systematic and flagrant violation of several clauses of the Unified Galactic Code, details of which I shall be giving you.

"And this—child, I think one must say," he concluded, turning, "is named Soraya. She doesn't understand much of what we are saying, which is hardly surprising. She wasn't brought up to speak pure Galactic, but an Irani dialect with some Galactic admixtures. She is, in fact"—and he looked straight at General Baden, wanting to see the full impact of his bombshell—"a native of ZRP Number Twenty-two, whose location we haven't yet established, but which narrows down to a thirty-parsec sphere now, and—"

"Twenty-two?" echoed the general in a strangled voice.

"But—" said both colonels simultaneously.

Langenschmidt let his face relax at last, into a beaming smile. "Have I your permission to explain my actions now?"

It had been decided at the last moment to make the closing session of the Conference on Non-Interference with Zarathustra Refugee Planets a public affair, with as much pomp and spectacle as Cyclopean resources could furnish at short notice, and full coverage by the planet's news services. There was much adulation of Omar Haust, the living representative of those who on untamed worlds struggled to wrest a precarious living from a hostile environment—at least, that was how Quist's speech compositor put it, and she was far too preoccupied to worry about the phrase herself. But there were some worried faces in the public seats, where Cyclopean notables, hurriedly summoned to show themselves, sat listening and scrutinising the offworld delegates arranged at a long table on the dais of the conference hall.

The matter troubling Quist was the same as it had been since she first yielded to Rimerley's irresistible bribe: would or would not the Corps leave enough salvageable material to balance the planetary budget this year, while they cast around for some other external revenue to replace what was being thrown away?

Gradually, through her mood of anxiety, a noise from outside the hall began to seep. She started, turning to gaze at the window which offered a view of the large square outside. There, thousands of the city's people were watching on public telescreens the proceedings of the conference.

They shouldn't be shouting like that. The thought briefly crossed her mind, and as it passed she leapt in amazement from her seat.

Down across the frame of the tall window a monstrous shining shape had moved, like a fish settling through clear water. A spaceship. A spaceship so large that the entire square was barely wide enough to afford it room.

Others in the hall had seen it go by, and the bewil-

dered speaker at the rostrum—one of the lesser delegates
from Earth, heaping praise on Cyclops for its noble self-
sacrifice—broke off his address. The shouting from outside turned to real screaming now.

The ranked notables started to get up, muttering in
alarm, and then the scene was frozen by the impact of
shock.

The tall main doors of the hall were slammed open—
not sliding back into the walls as they were meant to
move, but simply hurled from their frames by a tremendous blow from the far side. Over them, with the stolid
tramp of machines, came what most of the people
present had never seen except in historical recordings: a
squadron of the Corps Galactica in full battle equipment,
armour tough enough to repel an energy bolt, so heavy
that it was driven by miniaturised fusion reactors mounted
at the back, and polished to more-than-mirror brilliance
in every band of the spectrum. The crazy reflections
rendered it almost impossible to focus on the wearers,
making them seem like nightmare illusions.

That was why Gus Langenschmidt had insisted it be
worn. He didn't expect any resistance fierce enough to
justify its actual use.

The squadron wheeled right and left and filed around
the hill, taking station to surround it entirely, and he
came in last of all, striding directly towards Quist where
she stood, petrified, among the offworld delegates.

He wanted to get his opening statement out before
any of the news technicians regained enough presence of
mind to switch off the exterior transmissions.

"Alura Quist," he said, and the words rang around the
hall like the knell of doom, "I am Commandant Gustav
Langenschmidt, a duly appointed executive of the Corps
Galactica, and I arrest you for complicity in the following violations of the Unified Galactic Code, to wit: murder with malice, murder by default, conspiracy to—"

The screaming and panic began then. Langenschmidt

paused; his squadron was fully briefed on how to handle this sort of trouble. It took only a few minutes to restore calm, with the local notables sitting white-faced in their chairs, their hands between their knees as though they were trying to shrink and become too small to be seen, the offworld delegates muttering frantic unanswerable questions to each other, and the places of the news technicians taken by Corpsmen to ensure that the transmissions would go on without a break.

Langenschmidt resumed. "Conspiracy to interfere with the autonomous development of a Zarathustra Refugee Planet, conspiracy with Aleazar Rimerley and Lors Heimdall and others to murder one Ekim Hakimi and dismember his corpse, and certain other charges."

He wheeled where he stood, knowing that two armoured men had stamped to Quist's side and pinioned her arms, and confronted the cowering Cyclopeans in the public seats. He had intercepted a list of those invited which was supplied to the news service, and knew that all those he would name were present.

"Sophy Alt, I charge you with conspiracy with Aleazar Rimerley and Lors Heimdall and others to kill one Mara Rustum and dismember her corpse. Don Ambonine, I charge you with conspiracy with the same parties to kill one Ali Qurab and dismember his corpse. Ved Conakry, I charge you—"

And so on, the entire miserable tale of Rimerley's rich clients and their miserable victims, until there were more than thirty men and women shivering with terror before him.

Then he handed the documents from which he had been reading to one of his men, threw back his helmet, and strode to the dais. With the entire attention of the planet riveted on him, he began.

"People of Cyclops, and in particular you offworld visitors who have come here to attend the conference I so rudely interrupted"—he gave them a a sidelong glance and saw they were listening as intently as everyone else—"I want to explain the story behind the shocking scene you have just witnessed.

"You all know about the Zarathustra Refugee Planets. You perhaps also know that many more—perhaps well over a million more—people escaped from the Zarathustra nova than we have to date accounted for.

"Well, we have learned in the past few days that another shipload survived, on a world whose existence was discovered by accident and not notified to my Corps. The discoverer was the captain of a tramp space-freighter, named Lors Heimdall. He was making a somewhat unusual journey along a route served by no regular space-lines, when the strain proved too great for his engines and he was forced to make an emergency landing to conduct repairs on a Class A—that's a tolerably habitable—planet in an unvisited system.

"There, he discovered the descendants of a group of Irani-stock Zarathustrans, making the best of what they had.

"He kept the discovery to himself and his crew, believing that in some way he would eventually be able to exploit this secret. Not long afterwards, his chance occurred. A certain Justin Kolb, celebrated on Cyclops for his part in an accident in space, required the replacement of his right leg. Although he was in the care of your planet's leading surgeon, Aleazar Rimerley, the facilities here were not adequate for full-scale limb regeneration, and sending a patient to a more prosperous world is costly.

"Heimdall went to Rimerley with a proposition. He could secure for Kolb a replacement graft, a limb matched closely to his own, for a fraction of the cost of regeneration; Rimerley could charge his client—not Kolb; Alura Quist was paying, out of your planetary funds—the cost of a regeneration, and Heimdall and Rimerley could split the surplus profit.

"Rimerley accepted the offer. And Heimdall secured the limb as promised, by a peculiarly unpleasant deception practised on the unfortunate inhabitants of his private ZRP.

"In the early days of their life there, they had instituted a humane system of quarantine for people suffering from disease beyond their limited resources to cure—and there were plenty of those. Volunteers acted as what they called Receivers of the Sick, to convey them away from their community and the danger of infecting others, and tended them until they recovered or died.

"This system was on the verge of disappearance—so often had the Receivers died of the same illness as their patients, the idea seemed no longer practical. But Heimdall set himself and his men up as a new team of Receivers, worming their way into the natives' confidence and taking away not the truly ill, whom they preferred to disregard, but those whose bodily characteristics rendered them suitable as suppliers of spare parts.

"For Rimerley had seen the possibilities in an unlimited supply of graft material. Not many people on Cyclops are rich, but those who are are disproportionately so, and as greedy for youth as for material wealth. As you have heard, no fewer than thirty people in this hall have enjoyed the fruits of Rimerley's butchery—new limbs, new eyes, new vital organs!

"It is being pleaded that they did no more than offer euthanasia to the hopelessly sick, a practice tolerated here and on most inhabited planets. This is not true. How do we know?

"You may have heard that the Corps base is under orders to close, ostensibly as a symbol of protest against non-interference with ZRP's." He twisted his mouth around the words, and knew the irony was not lost on his hearers. "You may have seen this as an idealistic gesture, since Cyclops can ill afford to lose the revenue from the base. Or you may equally have wondered what possessed Alura Quist to issue her ultimatum.

"She issued it because Rimerley offered her a bribe: a new lease of life. He knew we were within sight of his secret; he thought to provide us with a distraction that would make our half-formed suspicions seem not worth the trouble of investigation. And the bait he dangled before Quist was the body, complete and healthy, of a young girl named Soraya: a source of new organs to replace her failing ones.

"That girl is alive—by a miracle—and in our hands. And she has told how, perfectly well, she was caused to appear to her friends as the victim of a fatal disease, a suitable subject for the ministrations of the Receivers of the Sick. She was not ill at all; she was not offered an easy death under the pretence that she was sick and incurable—she was simply shipped to Cyclops like an animal to the slaughter."

Langenschmidt paused. "People of Cyclops, it is no part of the Corps's duty to tell you what you should do. But I have worked on your planet for many years, and come to know you at least a little. I am sure you will *know* what you should do."

He turned to look at the pale, trembling conference delegates. "And as for you," he said, "I hardly need say that you have seen a Zarathustra Refugee Planet 'interfered with'. Think it over. And—go home."

For long moments, no one moved. Then, as if in a dream, the old man from ZRP One, Omar Haust, stood up and approached Quist. He looked at her as though at something disgusting found under a stone. Pursed his lips. Spat full in her face.

Langenschmidt snapped his helmet back over his head and gave the signal to his men. They left their stations and went to take hold of the men and women named in the long criminal indictment. Some passive and hopeless, some struggling and yelling hysterically, they were led away.

Last of all, with Langenschmidt at her heels, Quist was taken to endure the execration of her planet's people as she was marched towards the waiting spaceship.

XXI

"Made up your mind about non-interference?" Langenschmidt said to Maddalena with a tone of false jocularity.

There was no attempt to match it in her reply—depressed, abstracted.

"Gus, that isn't fair. Cyclops isn't a typical civilised planet, and come to that Heimdall and Rimerley aren't typical Cyclopeans."

"Granted." He looked down from the wall-length window of his villa towards the base, now back in full operation after the cancellation of the evacuation. "On the other hand, they do seem to be typical of those who get power, get influence, get wealth simply because they desire them so greedily. Truly civilised people don't crave power. They have—what would one call it?—empathy, perhaps, which holds them back."

"There's another and much older word," Maddalena said.

"Which is?"

"Conscience." Maddalena stirred as though unable to find a comfortable position on the luxuriously padded seat she was using. "But look at it another way, Gus. It's also empathy which makes me curse when I remember all the poor sick and crippled people I saw on Thirteen—in twenty solid years, remember. You've never had an on-planet assignment lasting longer then weeks or months. We ought to fix a limit—we ought to say if these people don't show signs of progress within such a time, we'll re-contact them openly and help them."

"Can we define progress?" countered Langenschmidt. "I thought that was one of the basic precepts behind non-interference. We must have lost our sense of direction if we can breed Heimdalls and Rimerleys on a so-called 'civilised world'. Maybe the ZRP's will re-discover what we've lost."

"I've heard all that," Maddalena snapped. "It still doesn't— Well, take a current conspicuous example. That poor girl Soraya had a boy-friend at home, and a sick mother. She was going to be married. We apply the non-interference rule strictly, and forbid her to return to her own planet with the memory of what she's seen since she was kidnapped. Precious little that must be, if she was kept in coma, but there the ruling stands, and I can't say I like it."

"In fact, you've chosen a bad example," Langenschmidt grunted. "Her adoring boy-friend accepted the payment Heimdall offered as a means of keeping the people eager to part with their sick kinfolk, took it home, and was promptly so well off he could take his pick of the eligible girls. And did, within the week."

"What? How do you know?" Disbelieving, Maddalena stared at him.

"Report came in a few hours ago. Using the information supplied by Heimdall's crew, a Corps party dressed themselves up as Receivers of the Sick and went to Soraya's home village. It's going to be a very useful disguise for our permanent agents, that—and I think you can rely on the non-interference rule being bent far enough to heal a really deserving case, now and again." He grinned maliciously. "Wouldn't like your next assignment to be a Twenty-two, would you? Or are you leaving the Corps?"

"No—no, I don't think so. Not yet." Maddalena's attention had been caught by two figures moving beyond the window: a youth and a girl both with long black hair. "Is that Bracy and Soraya out there?"

"Haven't you noticed how much time they're spending together? I took Bracy aside and told him what she'd

been through, and gave him his first Corps assignment—
looking after her. Not that he needed orders."

"He's already had his first Corps assignment. With
me."

"He hadn't even applied for probationary status
then—except verbally, to Nole, and that doesn't count.
This time it's official: rehabilitation of victim of criminal
assault."

Maddalena laughed, and the sound was gratifyingly
unforced to Langenschmidt's keen ears. "Damn you,
Gus! Why do you have to be such a nice guy?"

"Long practice," he retorted. "When you reach my
age—"

"You're also an idiot, but that must be congenital."
Maddalena's face clouded again. "Seriously, you know
. . . I had had it in mind to apply for another on-planet
posting. In spite of what I said when I first came here.
But I feel I wouldn't be able to tackle the job objective-
ly. I've been so submerged in dirt and disease and stupidity and barbarism I'm in danger of thinking of galactic
civilisation as the next thing to paradise. Well, I guess in
some senses it is, but it isn't *my* idea of paradise. Not
basically."

She paused and looked directly at him.

"Gus, I'd like to postpone my leave. I can, if I wish. I
don't much want to go back to Earth—if I was attached
to my home world, I'd never have left it in the first
place. At this distance it seems like an illusion. But
planets like Cyclops are all too real. Could you bear to
have me on your staff—say for a year—while I catch up
on reality by degrees?"

"I'd be honoured," Langenschmidt said. "Do you
know something? Long ago—I hadn't thought of it in
years until I spoke to Pavel Brzeska the other day—I told
him I thought you were going to make history eventually, and I'd like to be around when it happened. Well,
twenty years passed and no history to speak of. And

then suddenly you orbit back into my sector and things happen. I want to thank you for staying your hand until I was present as a witness and could have my wish granted."

"You're a sweetheart," Maddalena said fondly, and put out her fingers to meet his.

10th Year as the SF Leader!
Outstanding science fiction

By John Brunner

- [ ] **THE WRONG END OF TIME** (#UE1598—$1.75)
- [ ] **THE AVENGERS OF CARRIG** (#UE1509—$1.75)
- [ ] **TO CONQUER CHAOS** (#UJ1596—$1.95)
- [ ] **TOTAL ECLIPSE** (#UW1398—$1.50)

By A. E. Van Vogt

- [ ] **THE WINGED MAN** (#UE1524—$1.75)
- [ ] **ROGUE SHIP** (#UJ1536—$1.95)
- [ ] **THE MAN WITH 1000 NAMES** (#UE1502—$1.75)

By Gordon R. Dickson

- [ ] **THE STAR ROAD** (#UJ1526—$1.95)
- [ ] **ANCIENT, MY ENEMY** (#UE1552—$1.75)
- [ ] **NONE BUT MAN** (#UE1621—$2.25)
- [ ] **HOUR OF THE HORDE** (#UE1514—$1.75)

By M. A. Foster

- [ ] **THE GAMEPLAYERS OF ZAN** (#UE1497—$2.25)
- [ ] **THE DAY OF THE KLESH** (#UE1514—$2.25)
- [ ] **WAVES** (#UE1569—$2.25)
- [ ] **THE WARRIORS OF DAWN** (#UJ1573—$1.95)

By Ian Wallace

- [ ] **THE WORLD ASUNDER** (#UW1262—$1.50)
- [ ] **HELLER'S LEAP** (#UE1475—$2.25)
- [ ] **THE LUCIFER COMET** (#UE1581—$2.25)

THE NEW AMERICAN LIBRARY, INC.,
P.O. Box 999, Bergenfield, New Jersey 07621

Please send me the DAW BOOKS I have checked above. I am enclosing
$_____ (check or money order—no currency or C.O.D.'s).
Please include the list price plus 50¢ per order to cover handling costs.

Name _____

Address _____

City _____ State _____ Zip Code _____
Please allow at least 4 weeks for delivery